The Rabbit Ate
My Flip-Flops

Other books by Rachel Elizabeth Cole

The Rabbit Ate My Homework
The Rabbit Ate My Hall Pass

Coming Soon

The Rabbit Ate My Snow Pants

Plus more *The Rabbit Ate My ...* books!

The Rabbit Ate My Flip-Flops

Rachel Elizabeth Cole

Illustrated by Deanna Dionne

Tangled Oak Press, 2015

ISBN: 9780991766772

Cover by Littera Designs

First Edition

Library and Archives Canada Cataloguing in Publication

Cole, Rachel Elizabeth, 1976-, author
    The rabbit ate my flip-flops / written by Rachel Elizabeth Cole; illustrated by Deanna Dionne.

Issued in print and electronic formats.
ISBN 978-0-9917667-7-2 (pbk.).--ISBN 978-0-9917667-6-5 (html)

    I. Dionne, Deanna, illustrator II. Title.

PS8605.O438R31 2015   jC813'.6

To Dad, Glenda, and Abigail

In memory of Molly

Table of Contents

1
Time to Go

I stare at my computer and sigh. On the screen, a picture of a super-cool looking space station hovers in front of a swirling alien planet and a vast starry background. Above it, in large glowing green letters it reads, "Galaxy Guilds: Connect. Construct. Conquer." Beneath it, a countdown timer ticks down the minutes. 20:42:16. Less than a day until the coolest game of the year—the game my best friend, Quentin, and I have been waiting ages to play—finally releases, and am I going to be around to play it? Nope.

I'm going to be stuck in a cramped travel trailer with my annoying little sister, Libby, and my grandparents in a campground in the middle of nowhere. Why? Because Mom has to go to a conference in Hawaii for her job at the insurance company and Dad is going, too. So that means nobody will be here to take care of me and Libby. And since Nana and Papa are going camping this week, they thought we should come with them. Oh, and did I mention this camping trip is an annual thing Nana and Papa do every year with a bunch of other old people they've known since Dad was a kid?

I sigh again.

Just then a Skype message chirps. It's Quentin.

Qchow99: Sup?

Me: Packing

Qchow99: Boo

Me: Yeah

Qchow99: Galaxy Guilds is gonna be so lame without u

Me: :(

Qchow99: Why u no ask ur mom and dad to stay with me?

Me: I did but they said no

Qchow99: :(

Me: Yeah

Qchow99: How long r u gonna be gone?

Me: A week

Qchow99: Lame

Me: Yeah

Qchow99: U gonna have wifi?

Me: Dunno

Qchow99: Lemme know if u do
Me: I will
Qchow99: Gtg
Me: Ok
Qchow99: Cya

I exit Skype and power off my computer. I was so excited last year when Dad let me have his old desktop from work, but now I wish I'd held out for a laptop instead. At least I could bring a laptop with me. There's got to be Wi-Fi somewhere. Maybe even at the campsite. At least I've still got my iPod. It won't be the same as having my computer and I can't play Galaxy Guilds, but I've got some games and music and books on it so I hopefully won't be totally bored. Even if I can't get online.

"Are you packed yet, Drew?" Mom sticks her head into my room. Her arms are full of clean laundry and several coat hangers are hooked over her elbow.

I glance at the half-empty suitcase on my bed. "I, uh, just about."

Mom's eyebrows scrunch together. "Seriously, Drew, I don't have time to pack for you. If you forget anything, you're going to have to do without it. Toothbrush, hairbrush, socks, underwear. And don't forget your bathing suit. Now hurry up. You still need to set up Tiny's pen." She turns and heads down the hall towards her bedroom.

I plop down on my bed. I do *not* want to pack. I do *not* want to go. But I know stalling won't do much except get me yelled at. I yank open my dresser, grab some clothes, and stuff them in the suitcase. I fetch my toothbrush from the bathroom, grab my pillow, stick my iPod in my pocket, and call it good. Other than a laptop, I can't think of anything else I'd want to bring with me anyway.

Then I head downstairs to take care of the rabbit. At least somebody gets to stay home this week.

🥕 🥕 🥕

I set the bowl I've just filled with water at the laundry room sink in the bottom of the pen and stand back to survey my handiwork. Litter box, check. Food bowls, check. Rack full of hay, check. Cat jingle ball, check. Toilet paper tube stuffed with newspaper, check. Doll's bed with fleece blanket, check. Only thing missing: Tiny himself.

"Tiny!" I yell up the stairs. "Come on, Tiny! I've got a treat for you!"

I listen for a moment. No thunder of rabbit feet galloping across the floor above me. No whiskery nose appearing at the top of the steps. Where is that silly animal?

I head up to the living room.

No Tiny on the couch, his usual hangout. No Tiny in the kitchen, waiting for the fridge to open. No Tiny asleep on my bed, either.

Libby.

I head for her room. Just as I suspected. My seven-year-old sister has the rabbit. She also has a giant duffel bag on her bed and is trying to squeeze the rabbit inside it. He doesn't seem too impressed with the idea as he keeps hopping out every time she tries to zip it up.

"Just what do you think you're doing?" I demand.

Libby looks up at me, her eyes going wide, then her lower lip pokes out. "We can't leave Tiny!" She gives me that look—the one she always gives Mom before she asks for a new Barbie doll.

"Oh, please, don't start. We cannot bring that rabbit camping. Nana and Papa have said he has to stay here."

"But he'll be cold and lonely and scared. He won't know where we are!" Libby's lip quivers.

"He'll be fine. He'll be safe and sound in his pen in the laundry room. He'll eat hay and poop in his litter box and will be as happy as a rabbit can be. Besides, Tabitha will come by and feed him and play with him every day." Tabitha is in my grade and knows all about rabbits. She has two pet rabbits, Lolly and Oscar. I used to think she was weird, since she likes to wear men's clothes and old shoes, but now we're pretty good friends. And *just* friends.

"But he doesn't know that!" Libby sets her hands on her hips, daring me to argue with her. "He might think we've left him. Like his last owners did!"

"He's a rabbit! He doesn't think like that!" I roll my eyes. "He'll be fine. Now come on. Let's go. Nana and Papa will be waiting for us."

As if on cue, Dad yells from downstairs, "Drew! Libby! Time to go!"

"Look, we need to go." I cross the room and hoist the rabbit off the bed. He plants his front paws on my shoulder and nibbles my hair. "Stop that, you crazy rabbit." I push his head away. "C'mon. I've got your pen set up really nice for you." He bumps my ear with his nose and his whiskers tickle. I carry him downstairs. Libby trails behind me, her lower lip jutting out.

In the laundry room, I set Tiny in his pen. He flips his ears at me and hops around the pen, first sniffing and then rubbing his chin on his litter box, food bowls, hay rack, and toys. He nudges the small, plastic cat ball with his nose, sending it jingling across the concrete floor. Then he sits on his haunches, cocks his head and looks up at Libby and me, one ear swivelling toward us like a satellite dish.

"What?" I say. "You've got everything you need right here. Okay, maybe not the couch. But you'll be fine. Stop looking at me like that."

He stands on his hind legs as if he's gauging the

height of the pen. Then he wiggles his tail and hops over to his hay rack and starts munching.

"See, Libby? He'll be just fine."

Libby doesn't say anything. She just stands there glaring at me, her arms crossed.

"Drew?! Libby?!" Dad's voice is louder, more impatient. "Your grandparents are waiting!"

"Coming!" I yell back. I nudge Libby. "Let's go."

She doesn't move. "I want to say goodbye to Tiny."

I sigh. "Suit yourself." I lean over and give the rabbit a scratch between his giant ears. "See you in seven days, rabbit. Be good." Then I run upstairs, leaving Tiny and Libby behind.

Dad meets me at the front door. "Where's your sister?"

"Saying goodbye to the rabbit."

"Well, she better hurry up or she's going to get left." He grabs the last suitcase from the front hall. "Got everything?"

I pat my pocket with my iPod. "I think so."

Outside, Papa is hooking the last bungee cord holding my bike in place onto the back of the travel trailer. He grabs the seat and gives it a good shake. "Well, that should do it," he says with a grin. "Ready to go, Drew?"

I force myself to smile back at him. "Yeah, I'm ready."

Dad is packing the car with the last of his and Mom's

suitcases. Mom is giving Nana a list of last-minute instructions for taking care of Libby and me. Nana puts a hand on Mom's shoulder. "It'll be all right, Jessica. We managed to raise Todd and his brother, remember?"

Mom gives Nana a weak smile. "I know, I just—"

"Can't stop being a mom?" Nana gives her shoulder a squeeze. "Go. Relax. Enjoy yourself. Wayne and I have got this."

"C'mon, Libby!" Papa calls. "Where is that girl?" I can tell the adults are getting fed up with her and we haven't even started driving yet.

"I'll go find her," Mom says. She's about to head into the house when Libby appears from around the far side of the trailer.

"There you are," Mom says. "It's time to go."

"I was making sure Tiny wouldn't be lonely."

"Tiny will be fine," Mom says. "Tabitha will be by to check on him after supper."

"You locked his pen, right?" Dad frowns at me.

"Yup." I nod my head, then glance at Libby. "It's locked, right?"

Libby rolls her eyes. "Yes, Drew."

"And you made sure he's got hay and water?" Dad says.

"I did," I say.

"All right, then. We need to get going if your mom and I are going to catch our flight."

Mom wraps Libby and me in a hug so big I feel like I'm going to suffocate. "Be good for your grandparents. You can send a text to Dad and me anytime you need to, okay?" Then she kisses us both on the cheek and lets us go.

Dad ruffles my hair. "Take care of your sister."

He lifts Libby into his arms and tickles her, making her squeal. "Take care of your brother."

Libby wraps her arms around his neck. "Bye, Daddy. Have fun in Hawaii."

Dad swings her around, making her squeal again, then sets her on the ground. "Bye, sweetheart."

"Well, then I guess we're off," Mom says.

Mom and Dad say goodbye to Nana and Papa, make sure the front door is locked, then climb into the car. We wave as they pull out of the driveway and don't stop until they turn the corner at the end of the street.

"All right, everybody aboard the Montgomery Express!" Papa booms.

Libby and I scramble into the back seat of the truck and buckle up.

Nana and Papa climb into the front and Papa fires up the engine.

"Okie doke. Off to Long Beach we go!" Papa says and we pull away from the curb.

I glance back at the house. I hope Tiny won't be too lonely without us.

2
"I Gotta Go!"

I have to go pee," Libby says.

We're not even twenty minutes down the Island Highway when she makes this announcement.

"Already?" Papa adjusts the rearview mirror so he's looking back at us.

"Didn't you go at the house?" Nana says.

"I forgot."

"Oh, Libby." Nana sighs.

"Can't it wait until we stop for lunch?" Papa says.

"I really gotta go!" Libby crosses her legs and scrunches up her face.

"All right. All right. Hang on. There's a spot I can pull off just ahead." Papa signals and then pulls the truck and trailer off to the side of the highway. "Be quick about it."

Nana passes back the key for the trailer. "Do you know how to work the toilet?"

Libby nods. "You step on the pedal on the floor."

"If you need any help, just let us know."

"I will." Libby unbuckles her seatbelt and practically launches herself out the door.

"And remember to wash your hands!" Nana calls after her.

"What about you?" Papa raises his bushy eyebrows at me in the mirror.

I shake my head. "I'm good."

"Well, we won't be stopping again until lunch in Coombs."

"I can wait."

A few minutes later, Libby returns to the truck.

"Ready now?"

"Yup!" She beams at Nana and Papa.

Papa puts the turn signal back on and we pull back onto the road.

But not even ten minutes later, Libby announces she has to go again.

"But you just went!" Papa exclaims. "Can't it wait until lunch?"

"No, I gotta go now!" Libby says, then leans forward and whispers loudly into Nana's ear. "It's number two."

Papa sighs and puts on the turn signal again. "Okay. We're stopping."

As soon as the truck comes to a stop, Libby vaults out of door.

"Don't forget to flush!" Nana says just as the door slams shut.

"I hope this isn't going to take very long." Papa pulls his glasses off and rubs the bridge of his nose. "We have to be there by three for check in."

"I'm sure Sheila will take care of it." Nana pats him on the arm. "She always takes care of everything."

For a little while, no one says anything. Papa drums his thumb on the steering wheel, whistling between his teeth. Nana pulls out a nail file. I watch her smooth one of her long nails. Every time I see her she's got her nails painted different. Today they're a dark rose colour with a small, sparkly, fake diamond in the centre of each one. I stare out the window at the cars and trucks zooming by on the highway.

"So, Drew." Nana turns around in her seat. "Are you ready to have some fun this week?"

"Sure." I shrug.

"C'mon now!" Papa says. "You've got to have a little more excitement than that! Campfires, s'mores, swimming, biking, sandcastle building. It's going to be great!"

I manage a smile. That does sound kind of fun. Maybe not Galaxy Guilds fun, but better than being stuck inside the trailer for seven days.

Papa checks his watch. "Where is that girl?"

"I'll go check on her." Nana opens the door, then stops. "Wait. Here she comes."

"About time," Papa says as Libby climbs back in the truck. "You fall in the toilet?"

"No!" Libby shakes her head, making her dark curls bounce. "I put the seat down."

"All righty then. Let's get this show on the road." Papa puts the truck in gear again.

Once we're speeding along the highway again, Nana turns around in her seat. "What's the first thing you want to do when we get to the campsite?"

"Make s'mores!" Libby says.

"I think that can be arranged." Papa nods. "But not till after dinner."

"What about you, Drew?" Nana looks at me.

I know what the first thing I want to do is: find out if the campground has Wi-Fi so I can Skype Quentin and get Galaxy Guilds updates. But I know that's not the answer Nana's looking for. I shrug. "Maybe go to the beach?"

"That sounds like fun." Nana smiles. "We'll have to see what Sheila has planned for us first."

Papa grins at me in the mirror. "I know what I'm looking forward to: a relaxing round of golf. You like golfing, Drew?"

"I've never tried it."

"Never golfed? Well, we'll need to do something about that!"

"Uh, sure?" I say.

"How long till we get there, Papa?" Libby asks.

Papa looks at his watch. "In about three and a half hours, not counting lunch."

I can see Libby doing the math in her head. "When do we stop for lunch?"

"We should be there in about an hour. Don't tell me you're bored already?"

"No, just wondering."

"Well, how about some music?" Nana says and pulls out a CD and slides it into the CD player. "I got this just for the trip."

Something that sounds almost like that hit song that was playing everywhere a couple years ago fills the truck. Then the singing starts—and it's kids. And they sound bad.

"What the heck *is* this music?"

Nana holds up the CD case. "You kids don't listen to the Mini Bops?"

"Uh, no."

Libby claps her hands. "My friend Stella has all of the Mini Bops albums." Then she starts singing along at the top of her lungs.

Ugh. I pull out my iPod. Fortunately, I've brought my own playlist. I plug in my earbuds, crank up some decent music, and stare out the window, willing the drive to go faster.

Four songs into my playlist, Libby says, "I have to go again."

"To the bathroom?" Nana says.

"Really, Libby?" Papa says.

"You just went!" I roll my eyes. This trip is never going to end.

"Well, I have to go again. *Really bad!*"

Papa sighs. "There's a rest stop just up ahead. We'll stop there. Hang on."

Papa takes the next exit and pulls the truck and trailer into the rest area.

Libby can't seem to sit still. She keeps wiggling and twitching.

"Geez, Libby. You gonna wet your pants?" I say.

Her eyes narrow. "No-o! I'm not a baby!"

Then I see it. Is that hay in her hair?

As soon as the truck stops, Libby is out the door.

"Y'know," I say, pulling out my earbuds, "since we're stopping, I think I will go, too."

"Good idea," Nana says. "We can't keep stopping every fifteen minutes."

"At this rate, we'll be setting up camp at midnight." Papa scowls.

I jump out of the truck and follow Libby to the trailer. I climb the steps and pull open the door. Just as

I step inside, Libby disappears into the bathroom and the lock clicks. I tiptoe past the kitchen and put my ear to the door.

"You are a naughty bunny," Libby says on the other side. "You spilled your water."

She couldn't have! She wouldn't! She has to be talking to herself! I knock on the door. "Libby?"

"Just a minute!"

"Libby, open the door!"

"You have to wait. I'm using the bathroom!" I hear rustling and a loud *THUMP*! then, "Sssshhh!" and then the toilet flushes.

"C'mon, Libby!"

The door opens a crack. "What?"

"I heard a thump," I say.

"I hit my head."

THUMP!

Libby's eyes get big. "Oh! Ouch!" Then she kicks the door. "It's just so small in here. I keep hitting things."

THUMP!

"C'mon, Libby, open up!"

Libby tries to stop me, but I push the door open, sandwiching her against the sink, and pull back the shower curtain. There, sitting in the tub, surrounded by a gazillion poops and a large puddle—which I really hope is just spilled water—is Tiny, wearing his harness. He stands on his hind legs and gives me his saddest look.

Unbelievable!

"I'm getting Nana and Papa."

"No, Drew, you can't tell!" Libby squeezes out from behind the door. "They'll make us take Tiny back home!"

"Nuh-uh. No way. No lies." I cross my arms. "I'm telling Nana and Papa and you've got nothing to blackmail me with this time." When we found Tiny in a box in the ditch this spring, Libby blackmailed me into hiding him in my bedroom closet. She knew I'd broken my bike and lied to Dad that it had been stolen. But not this time. I learned my lesson. Nothing but the truth from now on.

Libby's lower lip starts to wobble and her eyes fill up with tears. "Please, please, *PLEASE!*"

"No! No way!" I gesture like a hockey ref signalling a no goal. "Libby, look at this place. This is a travel trailer. How are you going to keep a rabbit hidden? Nana and Papa will find him in a nanosecond. And I'm not getting blamed for it, either." With that I spin around and march out of the trailer and back to the truck.

Nana opens the door as I approach. "Everything all right?"

"I think you need to come here for a minute," I say.

"Oh," Nana says, already getting out of the truck.

Papa follows, looking concerned. "Is Libby okay?"

"She's fine," I say. Though probably not for long.

3
You Can't Bring a Rabbit Camping

Nana, Papa, and I are squeezed into the small hallway outside the trailer bathroom. Libby is still inside, sitting on the toilet, looking like she might burst into tears at any second. Tiny is still in the tub, looking rather displeased with all of us.

"What on earth would make you think bringing Tiny would be a good idea?" Papa says, running a hand through his thinning hair.

"You can't bring a rabbit camping," Nana says. "There are dogs and bears and eagles..."

"He could get hurt!" Papa says.

"He could get lost!" Nana adds.

"And where are we going to keep him?" Papa finishes.

"Oh, Libby." Nana shakes her head.

"But Tiny will be lonely and scared all by himself at home!" Libby protests.

"He's a rabbit!" Papa exclaims.

"But what if something bad happens? No one will be there to help him." Tears start running down Libby's cheeks.

"Oh, Libby," Nana says again, rummaging in her pocket for a Kleenex. "What are we going to do with you?"

Papa checks his watch. "Do either of you have a house key?"

"Um, at home," I say. "I forgot it."

Libby just shakes her head no and blows her nose.

"Do we even have time to take him home, Wayne?" Nana says.

Papa frowns. "Not if we want to check in any time close to three."

"So we're not taking him home?" I say, not sure if I'm feeling relieved or annoyed. I mean, I'm kind of excited to bring Tiny with us. Camping will definitely be less boring now. But I'm kind of annoyed Libby is getting her way.

Again.

Papa sighs. "No. The rabbit is coming with us."

Libby lets out a cheer so loud it makes Tiny thump.

Now that Tiny has been discovered, Nana and Papa call Mom and Dad to let them know we have the rabbit. They call Tabitha, too. Then they bring him into the truck with us. Nana puts a towel between Libby and me and puts Tiny on top of it.

"Make sure he stays put," she says.

She doesn't need to worry. As soon as the truck starts moving, Tiny's eyes bug out like they're going to pop out of his head and he flattens himself against the seat and stays that way for the rest of the drive.

For lunch, we go through the Triple O's drive-thru instead of stopping at the Coombs Country Market as planned.

"See the goats on the roof?" Nana says as we drive past the sprawling market.

"No, where?" Libby says, gawking out the window.

"There." I point. "On the big grass roof."

"I don't see them."

"THERE! They're right there." I point again. "You're going to miss them."

"Did you see them, Libby?" Nana says after we've passed.

"I missed them." Libby pouts.

"We'll try to stop for ice cream on the way back," Papa promises.

A little further down the road we wind past a big lake and drive into the woods. The fir trees on the sides of the road get bigger and bigger until they are so huge they look like wooden skyscrapers. I gaze up at them through the truck window. Now I know what the old stump in the woods by our house must've looked like before they cut it down all those years ago.

A sign tells us we've entered Cathedral Grove. I've never been in a cathedral. The closest I've come is the big church in Victoria where Uncle Shawn and Aunt Sophie got married. It's nothing compared to this forest.

As we pass a parking lot on the side of the road full of cars and campers and trucks with trailers, Libby says, "I want to see the big trees, Papa. Can we stop? Please?"

I want to stop, too. I can see people walking on trails that weave between the humongous trees. They look like ants. I want to see if all four of us can wrap our arms around one of the tree's trunks like I've seen people do in old pictures.

"On the way home," Papa replies. "We would stop, but we're running late."

Bummer.

Just outside Port Alberni, I hear sirens. So does Papa. He looks in the rearview mirror and lets out a loud sigh. "Hang on," he says. "We're getting pulled over."

Papa signals and pulls the truck and trailer to the side of the road. He rolls down the truck window and a few seconds later a policeman walks up.

"Do you know what the speed limit is through this section?" he asks.

"Eighty?" Papa says.

"Try sixty."

"Oh."

The policeman takes Papa's license and registration and disappears back to his patrol car. He comes back a little later with the papers and a speeding ticket. "Drive careful now," he says.

As we pull back onto the road, Papa checks his watch and sighs again.

While we stop for gas in Port Alberni, Nana tells us how there was a big tsunami that hit the town when she was a girl. "Houses were washed off their foundations and some even floated into the inlet. But no one died because there was enough warning. They used taxicabs to drive everyone to safety."

"Wow," I say, glancing around at the streets and buildings. Everything seems so normal, it's hard to imagine what it must've looked like after a tsunami.

"But we aren't by the ocean," Libby says.

"The inlet is the ocean," I say.

"I know that." Libby crosses her arms and glares at me.

"The water came all the way from the ocean, up the inlet, and into town," Nana explains. "Because the inlet is narrow, it made the wave so high it was strong enough to wash away whole streets. It was such a mess afterward." She shakes her head at the memory.

"What if there's a tsunami while we're camping?" Libby says, her eyes getting round.

"Don't worry." Nana smiles reassuringly. "They have sirens that will go off so everyone can get away safely."

"Even Tiny?" Libby cuddles the rabbit.

"Even Tiny." Nana nods.

Just as we are leaving Port Alberni, Libby announces, "I need to use the bathroom. For real this time."

Papa doesn't say a word as he puts the turn signal on, but I can see the muscle in his jaw clenching.

🥕 🥕 🥕

It's past four o'clock when we pull into the Wind & Tide Beach Resort and Campground. We park outside the office and Nana and Papa go in. A few minutes later they come out. Papa doesn't look too happy.

"What's the matter, Papa?" Libby says.

Papa doesn't reply. He just gets in the truck and slams the door. Nana doesn't say anything, either. Papa puts the truck into gear and we lurch forward. We follow the winding road past campsites full of trailers and campers and tents. Then the road forks. A sign that says "Beach Access" points to the left.

Another that says "Outhouses" points to the right. We turn right. Great. Now I know what Papa was scowling about.

The road keeps taking us further and further away from the beach. The trees get thicker and thicker until the warm sun seems a distant memory. Finally, Nana says, "Here it is. Number 105." We pull up in front of a campsite surrounded by dense evergreen trees right next to the outhouses. On the opposite side of the road, there's a swampy bog.

"We really need to talk to Sheila," Papa grumbles. "She told us she'd reserved beachfront sites for the whole group. We're supposed to be on the beach, not the farthest thing from it!"

"I'm sure we can get it sorted out tomorrow." Nana pats Papa's arm, but I can tell she's irritated, too.

"Well, we better park this rig. We have to stay somewhere tonight." With some fancy steering Papa backs the trailer into the campsite. "All right. Everyone sit tight while I unhitch the trailer." He hops out and goes around back. He comes back a few minutes later with his shirt collar up. He swats away some bugs and climbs back into the cab. "You brought bug spray, right?" he says to Nana.

"Of course." She nods. "It's in the trailer."

"We're going to need it," he says through gritted teeth. "This place is crawling with mosquitos."

I glance out the window just as a mosquito lands on it. A big one.

This trip is going from bad to worse.

4
"Out, Out, Out!"

Once Papa gets the trailer set up, I grab Tiny, and then we all jump out of the truck and make a run for the trailer before the mosquitos can get us.

"In, in, in!" Nana says, as we race up the steps and inside. She slams the screen door shut behind us before any mosquitos can follow us inside.

"Nasty little bloodsuckers," Papa mutters.

Libby sits on the couch. I set Tiny on the floor and sit down beside her. Tiny gives a little shiver, then begins hopping around, investigating the trailer. With the side of the trailer that has the couch and table slid out, it's actually pretty roomy. At the front there's Nana and Papa's bedroom. Then the kitchen, dining table, and couch in the middle. And, at the back, is the bathroom and two bunks for Libby and me.

Where we will put the rabbit is the only problem.

"He can sleep with me!" Libby says.

"Is that your solution for everything?" I roll my eyes.

Libby gives me a look that could freeze icebergs.

"No loose rabbits," Papa says. "There are too many things for him to get into."

"We'll just have to drive into Tofino and get him a cage," Nana adds.

"You can't put Tiny in a cage!" Libby says, horrified.

"Well, we need to put him somewhere!" Papa says. "Doesn't he have a pen at home?"

"Yeah, a puppy pen. Mom got it just for this trip."

"Then we'll get a pen."

"You won't find a cage big enough anyway," I say.

In the three months we've had him, Tiny has grown from a tiny baby to a giant rabbit. Tabitha has said he can grow until he's a year old and can weigh up to twenty pounds. Right now he weighs fourteen pounds and is almost as big as Quentin's cocker spaniel.

"And he needs hay and rabbit pellets and a litter box," Libby says. "And vegetables. He loves salad."

"Definitely the litter box," I say. "Tiny is leaving a trail."

"What?!" Nana says, her eyes widening as she spots the handful of poops Tiny has left on the carpeted floor. Then Tiny stands on his hind legs and chomps one of the kitchen cabinets. "Out!" she shrieks. "Out, out, out!"

"But Nana! There's mosquitos!" Libby protests.

"We'll be eaten alive!" I add.

Nana turns and opens a cabinet door. She pulls out a container of OFF! insect repellent and hands it to me. "Now put his leash on him and take him out. When we get a cage, then he can come back inside."

And just like that, Libby, the rabbit, and I find ourselves back out in the mosquito-infested woods. The *stinky* mosquito-infested woods.

"What is that smell?" Libby says, wrinkling her nose.

"That would be the outhouses." I cover my mouth with the front of my tee shirt and try not to breathe too deeply. In the warm afternoon air, the smell is overpowering.

"Yuck."

I want to say, "You can say that again," but that would mean opening my mouth. Smelling outhouses is bad enough. Tasting them? I'd rather eat liver and onions for a month. Raw.

A few seconds later, Nana and Papa come out of the trailer. "Stay around the campsite. We'll be back soon." They hop in the truck and drive off.

I swat at a mosquito. "I don't think this stuff is working."

"Me either." Libby makes a face, waving away a swarm that's circling her head. "I bet there aren't any mosquitos at the beach. And I bet it doesn't smell like outhouses."

"We can't go to the beach! You heard what they said! We have to stay here."

"I *know*, Drew."

I put Tiny on the ground.

"Can I hold the leash?" Libby asks.

"You're not going to leave the campsite, right?"

"I won't. I promise."

"Well, okay then." I hand it over.

She loops the leash around her wrist to shorten it and follows Tiny as he goes hopping and stopping, hopping and stopping around the picnic table.

I pull out my iPod. I can play Mega Velocity while we wait for Nana and Papa to get back. I swat another mosquito and sit on the picnic table. These mosquitos are ridiculous. I pull the neck of my tee shirt up and loop it over the tops of my ears. I'm sure it looks stupid, but better than smelling outhouses or being a mosquito buffet.

"Look, Drew!" Libby squeals.

I glance up. At the edge of the campsite, there's a small brownish-grey squirrel hopping through the brush. It stops when it sees Tiny. Tiny also spots the squirrel. His giant ears swivel forward and he stretches forward on his tiptoes, his nose going a mile a minute.

The squirrel chatters and shakes its tail at Tiny. The rabbit doesn't move. Then the squirrel runs at Tiny. The rabbit still doesn't move. At the last second the squirrel stops, turns, and runs up the nearest tree. It perches on a branch and chatters angrily at Tiny, twitching its tail. Then it hurls a pine cone at him. It lands within inches of the rabbit's nose, making him jump.

For a moment, Tiny crouches there on the ground, not sure what to do.

"It's okay, Tiny," Libby says, reaching for him.

Then the squirrel throws another pine cone. Tiny takes off running. Libby's arm is almost pulled out of its socket trying to keep up with him. "Tiny! Slow down!"

"Libby! Don't let go!" I yell.

"I can't!" Libby screams. "My hand is stuck! Help, Drew!"

I jump up and chase after them. "Tiny, stop! Stop!"

Tiny gallops straight through the woods with poor Libby being dragged behind. I race after, dodging trees and ferns and jumping over fallen logs and rocks. Ahead of me the rabbit and Libby burst out of the forest next to the outhouses, startling a man carrying a roll of toilet paper. He jumps back as they rush by. Finally, they come to a stop on the gravel trail. Libby drops onto the ground beside the rabbit, wraps her arms around his neck, and starts to cry.

I catch up with them. Tiny is breathing hard and the whites of his eyes are showing. "Don't strangle him," I say.

Libby just keeps sobbing. "You scared me so much, Tiny."

"Don't cry, Libby. He's okay." I don't want to admit it, but he really scared me, too. I help Libby stand. She's got a scratch on her leg that's bleeding and she could use a Band-Aid. "C'mon, let's get back to the campsite, before Nana and Papa get back."

I grab Tiny and head down the trail back to the road, Libby following behind, still holding the leash and sniffling. On the main road, we run into a man and woman walking their pug-nosed dog. "Whoa! That's a big bunny!" the man says.

"He's a Flemish Giant," I say.

"You got the giant part right!" he says.

We round the bend in the road and our campsite comes into view. My arms are getting tired from carrying Tiny, so I put him down and take the leash from Libby. "Don't run off again," I say, pointing. "Home is that way."

Tiny seems to know and starts hopping toward the campsite. Libby and I follow him all the way back to the trailer. He stops when we reach the picnic table again. Then he sniffs the ground and flops down on his belly and kicks his legs out to the side of him.

"Who brings a rabbit camping?" a voice behind us says.

Libby and I spin around. Two boys—twins, actually—maybe a year or two younger than me, are standing on the road at the edge of our campsite. They're both short and skinny and have the same shaved brown hair and the same ears that stick out from the sides of their heads. And they both have the same sneer on their freckled faces. The one on the right sets his hands on his hips. The one on the left crosses his arms. Between them stands a stocky white dog with huge drooly jowls and a brown patch over its right eye. It looks about as mean as they do.

"Um, we do," I say, wishing yet again I had Quentin's talent for smart comebacks.

"We can bring our rabbit camping if we want to," Libby says. "There's no law."

"Well, there should be. Rabbits are dumb," the one on the right says.

"Why don't you get a real pet?"

"Rabbits aren't dumb!" Libby juts out her chin. "Tiny is the smartest rabbit. He can do rabbit agility. What can your dog do?"

"Our dog can eat your rabbit!"

"That's not funny!" Libby scowls at them.

"You're hungry, aren't you, Moose?" the one on the left says to the dog.

Moose barks and lunges forward, straining against his leash.

Tiny pulls his feet underneath him, looking ready to run again. I tighten my hold on the leash. "Look, just leave us alone," I say.

"Make us."

"Yeah. What you gonna do? Sic your bunny on us?" The one on the left pretends to shake in fear. "I'm so scared!"

"No! But we'll tell our Papa on you." Libby wags a finger at them.

"Let it go, Libby," I say, putting a hand on her shoulder. "They're just jerks."

"I heard that!" the one on the right says. "If we're such jerks, why are you the one calling people names?"

"Yeah, you're the jerks," his brother adds.

"Fine. We're jerks," I snap. "Now why don't you go

away and leave us jerks to do our jerk thing." I steer Libby towards the trailer. "C'mon."

"Get the bunny, Moose!"

"Get him! Get him!"

Moose starts barking like crazy.

Libby throws herself on top of the rabbit. "Drew! Do something!"

A burst of adrenaline shoots through my veins. "You better not let that dog off his leash!"

"Or what? What are you gonna do about it?"

"I'll … I'll …" I glance around quickly for something to defend us with. My gaze falls on the cubby in the side of the trailer where Papa stores his tools and things. It's propped open and I see his golf club set lying next to the tool box. I reach inside and pull out a golf club with a big metal head. "If you let your dog near our rabbit, I will use this on him. I promise you I will." To make my point, I swing the club through the air—and accidentally hit the side of the picnic table. *CLANG!* The handle breaks off right in my hands. The metal part of the club falls to the ground with a *THUMP!*

The twins burst out laughing.

"Just get out of here!" I yell at them. I scoop up the rabbit, grab Libby's arm, and haul both of them into the trailer, letting the door slam behind us.

Outside, I hear the twins still laughing as they walk off down the road with their dog.

I hope we never see them again.

"You okay, Libby?" I say.

"Yeah," she sniffles. "You're okay, too, aren't you, Tiny?"

"He's fine," I say and set him on the floor. He flips his ears and hops over to Libby. She scratches him between the ears and he nose-bumps her hand.

I peek out the screen door. The twins seem to be gone, so I go back outside and retrieve the pieces of Papa's golf club. Papa is going to kill me. Now what am I going to do? I slump on the picnic table. This trip has gone from bad to worse to downright horrible.

I hold the handle in one hand and the metal shaft in the other. It looks like I can slide the shaft into the handle. Maybe with a bit of glue or duct tape it'll be okay? I stick the club back together and put it in the bag. I'll tell Papa about it later. Much later.

Libby pokes her head out the screen door. "Um, Drew? We have a problem."

I groan. "Please don't tell me Tiny ate something."

"No, not Tiny."

Inside, Tiny is lounged on the couch, looking very much like he does every day at home. He turns an ear in my direction, but otherwise doesn't move a muscle.

Libby leads me to the bathroom. "It won't flush," she says.

"What do you mean?"

She opens the lid. It is full to the top with brown water and toilet paper.

"Gross!"

"Can you make it flush?"

"You've got more experience with this toilet than I do!"

Libby's lip wobbles.

I step on the pedal on the floor. The water rises another inch so it's dangerously close to overflowing the bowl. "Uh, I'm sure Papa knows how to fix it," I say. At least, I sure hope so.

The idea of using those stinky outhouses makes my stomach turn.

5
The Cage

"What is the rabbit doing inside?" Nana says when she and Papa get back.

Libby and I are sitting on the couch, playing Go Fish with Libby's Disney Princess playing cards. Tiny is lounged between us, his head on his paws, eyes half shut.

"Some mean kids said they'd let their dog eat Tiny," Libby says. "Got any eights, Drew?"

"Go fish," I say, nodding my agreement. "They were real jerks."

Nana sighs. "This is why we said you couldn't bring the rabbit."

"Who were these kids? What campsite are they in? I'll go talk to their parents," Papa says.

"I don't know," I say. "They have a big white dog."

"His name is Moose," Libby adds.

"Well, if you see them again, let us know."

"We will."

Nana mutters something about children today. "Okay," she says brightly. "How about you two pack up your game and help Papa unload the bunny things. I'll get dinner started."

Libby and I put the cards away and then follow Papa out of the trailer. He opens the back door of the truck and pulls out a large box.

"This is a *cage*!" Libby says.

"Beggars can't be choosers," Papa says. "Nana wanted something with a bottom on it. Now you carry the bag of shavings."

"Shavings? He's not a hamster! Didn't you get him a litter box?"

"This cage isn't much bigger than a litter box," I say. At home, Tiny has an extra-large cat litter box in the kitchen. This cage would fit inside it.

Libby scowls at me. "That's not funny, Drew."

"I wasn't trying to be funny," I say. "At least they got the right kind of pellets." I pull out a pink and purple bag of Martin's Timothy rabbit food.

"But where's the hay?" Libby says.

"Do you know how much the pet store wants for a bitty bag of hay?" Papa says. "He can eat grass."

"But he needs hay!" Libby protests.

"Grass *is* hay. Remember, Libby?" I don't mention there's not much grass in the forest. But maybe there's some down at the beach. If we can get Tiny there without running into a certain dog and its owners. "It's just for a week. He'll be okay."

"Come on, Libby," Papa says. "Help us carry everything in."

Libby doesn't say anything as Papa and I lift the box and carry it up the stairs. I'm just through the door when I hear a *SPLOOSH!* and then a shriek from the bathroom.

The door bursts open. Nana rushes out and starts grabbing towels from the cupboard and throwing them on the growing brown puddle on the floor. "Wayne! We've got a flood!"

I catch the look on Libby's face. She looks like she's about to cry. I actually feel bad for her.

Once Nana mops up the bathroom floor, she takes the towels down to the laundry to wash them. Papa grabs his tools and heads to the bathroom. We've finished putting the cage together, except for the little plastic shelf. We've left that off. Tiny would never fit on it anyway. Libby fills the bottom of the cage with shavings and clips the food and water bowl to the bars. She really doesn't look happy about Tiny's new living space. To tell the truth, neither am I. He's used to having the run of our whole house. He's not going to like spending a week in this shoebox of a cage.

"We'll just have to take him for a walk every day," I tell her.

"But what about Moose?"

"It's a big campground. We should be able to stay away them."

Libby doesn't look convinced.

Tiny hops down off the couch to investigate the cage. He sniffs it all over, then pokes his head through the small door in the side.

"I don't think he's gonna fit," I say.

But he does. He squeezes through the opening and into the cage. He heads straight for the bowl of rabbit pellets and starts gobbling them up like he hasn't eaten all day. Come to think of it, he really hasn't. When he's done, he sniffs around the cage, then pees in the corner. Then he makes like he's going to hop back out, so I close the door. He bumps his nose against the door, then grabs the bars with his teeth and gives it a shake. *RATTLE! RATTLE!* He gives me an annoyed look.

"Sorry, Tiny," I say. "You've got to stay inside the cage now." His pen at home must seem like a mansion compared to this.

41

Papa comes out of the bathroom, grumbling. "Well, I don't think the toilet is going to get fixed tonight. Not sure what's the matter with it, but it won't flush. Looks like I'll be running into town to the hardware store tomorrow."

"But what if we have to go to the bathroom?" Libby says.

"Then you can use the outhouse." Papa shrugs.

Ugh.

"Well, I see you've got Tiny set up now. How about we go spark up the grill, Drew?"

"Uh, sure."

Papa shows me how to light the barbecue, then we fetch a package of Bavarian smokies from the fridge and put them on the grill.

"Nana should be back soon," he says, closing the lid. "And then we can eat."

Eventually, Nana returns with her arms full of clean towels. "Did you get the toilet fixed?"

Papa shakes his head. "Hopefully tomorrow."

"At least we're close to the outhouses," Nana says.

We are definitely close to the outhouses. Right now I can smell them. Even from inside the trailer.

Nana puts the towels away in the cupboard and we sit down to dinner at the dining table.

I slather my smokie with ketchup, mustard, and an extra helping of relish, and then spoon Nana's potato salad onto my plate. I didn't realize how hungry I was until now.

"Why aren't you eating, Libby?" Nana says.

"Do we have any salad?" Libby plays with her fork.

"This *is* salad!" I say, scooping potato salad into my mouth. "And good salad, too."

"No, the lettuce kind."

Oh, *right*. I glance at Tiny in his cage. He's got his nose stuck through the bars, looking sad. "Yeah, lettuce salad would be good, too."

"Maybe tomorrow night," Nana says. "I didn't know you kids were such salad lovers."

I grin at Libby. "Oh, we *love* salad."

She grins back.

"After dinner how about we roast some marshmallows?" Papa says.

"What about the mosquitos?" I say, scratching one of the red welts on my legs. *OFF!* seems to mean *ON!* to these mosquitos.

"The smoke will keep the mosquitos away." Nana nods. "Now eat up. No marshmallows if you don't eat all your dinner."

After we eat, Libby and I help clear away the dishes. Nana washes and Papa dries.

"Knock! Knock!" A woman with bright blond hair, large sunglasses, and pink lipstick is standing outside the screen door. Over her shoulder she's got a large pink bag. A tiny Chihuahua, almost the same colour as the lady's hair, pokes its quivering nose out the top, blinking. "Anybody home?"

"Yes, we are!" Nana holds open the door and the woman climbs inside. Behind her is a short, balding man with a mustache and glasses. He's wearing black socks with brown sandals. The socks are pulled up to his knees.

"Sheila! Ralph! Long time no see!" Papa says, towelling a plate and handing it to me to put away.

"Everyone getting settled in?" Sheila asks, her gaze bouncing from Nana to Papa to me and Libby and finally onto Tiny in his cage. "Oh, I see you've really brought everyone along, haven't you?"

"Tiny was a last-minute addition," Papa says.

"Tiny?" Ralph laughs. "He could feed a small village."

"Tiny's not food!" Libby says.

"I'm sure Ralph is joking, dear," Nana says.

"Of course I'm joking," Ralph says. Then he sneezes, "*ACHOO!*"

THUMP!

We all look at Tiny. His giant ears are straight up in the air, his eyes showing the whites.

THUMP!

Libby runs to the cage. "It's okay, Tiny." She opens the door and pets him until he calms down.

"I do hope the bunny isn't going to interfere with our schedule," Sheila says, stroking her dog's head. "We've got a lot planned this week."

"He shouldn't be a problem," Nana assures her. "The kids will take care of him."

"They can't stay here at the campsite the whole time. I've got some wonderful things planned for them, too."

"Like swimming?" Libby says.

"Well, no."

"Surfing?" I say.

"Er, not that."

"Mountain biking?"

"No."

"Sandcastles?"

"No."

"Well, then what?" Libby says.

"It's a surprise." Sheila smiles at Libby and me like we're both kindergartners. "But it'll be lots of fun!"

If this surprise turns out to be finger painting, I'm taking the rabbit and hitchhiking home.

"*ACHOO!*" Ralph sneezes again.

THUMP! Tiny thumps again.

Nana offers Ralph a Kleenex. He blows his nose. *HONK!*

THUMP!

"You're scaring Tiny!" Libby says.

"Ugh! My allergies," Ralph says. "I think I'm allergic to your rabbit." He sneezes again. "*ACHOO!*" He buries his face in the Kleenex and stumbles out of the trailer. "I'll be waiting outside."

"Well," Sheila says, "I guess we should be getting going. We just wanted to stop by and make sure you were settling in okay."

"About that," Papa says. "I thought we were all getting beachfront sites."

"Yes, well, I'm really sorry about that." Sheila purses her lips. "They assured us we'd have three beachfront sites. I'd said we'd prefer them all together, but if they weren't that was all right, too. But when we arrived this morning, they only had the two beach sites together." Sheila shakes her head. "They've assured us the moment another beachfront site opens up you'll be moved there. I was told Wednesday at the latest, but possibly before that."

Ugh. Three more days stuck in the woods a mile away from the beach, smelling outhouses and dodging mosquitos? Double ugh.

Nana gives Papa a look that says pretty much exactly what I was just thinking. "I guess all we can do is wait."

"Hopefully a site comes available sooner than later." Papa sighs.

"Let's hope so!" Sheila gives Nana a winning smile.

"All right. So, we'll see you all tomorrow at nine for the pancake breakfast?"

Nana and Papa assure her we'll be there at nine sharp. Then Sheila puts her sunglasses back on and heads outside to join her husband.

After they leave, Papa says, "So how about those marshmallows?"

Libby claps her hands. "Can we bring Tiny outside?"

"Sure."

"Coming Drew?"

"Yeah, just a sec." I grab my suitcase, pull out a pair of jeans, a long-sleeved shirt, and a pair of socks. Too bad I didn't think to bring a pair of gloves or a scarf. I quickly change in the bathroom and head outside. It's getting late and our campsite has already lost the sun. The last few rays are slanting through the trees, leaving a few patches of golden light on the ground.

Nana and Libby are sitting in lawn chairs around the fire pit. They're both wrapped in beach towels. Libby is holding Tiny's leash. The rabbit has his paws on the rim of the metal fire pit, sniffing the newspapers Papa has balled up inside it. Papa is digging around in a cubby at the back of the trailer.

"Grab a seat, Drew," he says. "Just gotta get some firewood."

I grab an empty lawn chair, swat at the mosquitos hovering in the air, and sit down.

Nana offers me a beach towel and I take it gladly. Even with a long-sleeved shirt and jeans, the mosquitos aren't giving up.

Libby grabs a marshmallow from the bag on the ground between her chair and Nana's and stuffs it in her mouth.

"Slow down, Libby," Nana says. "If you eat them all now, there'll be none for the fire."

"Sorry, kids," Papa says. "Looks like there isn't going to be a fire tonight."

"What?" I say.

"Why?" Libby says.

"The firewood got a little soggy." He drops a few pieces of wet wood onto the ground. It smells like outhouse. "The flood got it."

"Oh, Wayne!" Nana says. "Is anything else damaged?"

"Fortunately, no. The wood seems to have got the worst of it."

"Awwwww..." Libby says.

"I'll get some more in the morning. We'll just have to roast marshmallows tomorrow night."

Nana swats a mosquito. "Come on, everybody. Let's head back inside. These mosquitos are getting persistent."

"That's putting it mildly," Papa says, smacking his arm.

6
Thump! Rattle! CRASH!

Libby and I have just finished our second game of Go Fish when Nana says, "Well, I don't know about you—" She yawns. "—but I'm about ready for bed."

"Pyjamas, you two," Papa says.

I grab my pyjamas and quickly change in the bathroom.

When I come out, Libby is already changed into a pink nightgown that says "Girl Power" on the front.

"Let's go use the outhouse," Nana says to Libby.

"I can hold it!" Libby says.

"No, you can't. Now come along." Nana ushers Libby out of the trailer.

"You should go, too," Papa says to me.

Ugh. As if smelling those outhouses all the way over here isn't bad enough.

I put on my hoodie and flip-flops and trudge down the road to the outhouses. I hold my breath and push open the door to the one marked "Men's." I can almost taste the smell, it's that strong. I lift the lid and gag. A big black hole gapes back at me and a fly buzzes up from inside it. I go as fast as I can, all the while trying to breathe as little as possible without passing out. Then I beat it out of the outhouse as fast as I can. Peeing is one thing, but if I gotta do the other, I'm begging one of our neighbours to let me in to use their bathroom.

When I get back to the trailer, I wash my hands and brush my teeth. Fortunately, the flood hasn't affected the sink.

I open the bathroom door, just as Libby and Nana are coming in.

"I call top bunk!" Libby says.

"No way! I'm older! I get top bunk!"

"Kids, kids." Nana sounds weary. "Why don't you flip a coin?" She pulls out her purse and hands me a quarter.

This is so unfair. I should get top bunk by default. There shouldn't even be a question. Grudgingly, I flip the coin and cover it with my hand. "All right, Libby. Call it."

"Heads!"

I lift my hand. Heads. Ugh.

Libby grabs her Princess blanket and pillow and

climbs up onto the top bunk. I squeeze onto the lower bunk. Stupid coin.

"All right, everyone. Lights out!" Papa calls from their room. Then he flicks out the lights to the trailer.

"Good night! Sweet dreams!" Nana calls.

"Good night!" Libby and I call back.

The trailer goes silent. A few moments later, I hear snoring start up from Nana and Papa's room. I sigh and roll over. There's a little window and I peek out through the curtains. It's pitch black outside except for a few faint orange blurs of fires at other campsites.

I pull out my iPod. As soon as the screen lights up I get a low battery warning. Better find my charger and plug it in. I sneak out of bed, grab my suitcase from under my bunk, and hunt through it. Where is my charger? Then I remember. My charger is still sitting on my bedstand at home! No! This can't be!

"Drew? What are you doing?" Libby whispers.

"Nothing," I mutter. I switch off my iPod and stuff it in my suitcase. Then I flop down in my bunk. Can this trip get worse?

THUMP!

"Tiny! Quiet!" I whisper.

THUMP!

The snoring at Nana and Papa's end of the trailer stops.

"Is that the rabbit?" Papa's sleepy voice grumbles.

"Tiny! Shhhh!" Libby says.

I climb out of bed and go to his cage. "Hey, it's okay. We're all here. Nothing to be afraid of."

THUMP!

"Can't we let him out? *Please?*" Libby says.

"Not a chance," Nana says. "There is just too much he'll get into!"

"But he'll sleep on my bunk the whole night!" Libby says.

"What if he needs to use the bathroom?" I say. "He can't jump from there."

"Then he can sleep with Drew! We'll leave the cage open so he'll be able to get back in and use the bathroom."

Nana stumbles out of the bedroom and flicks on the light over the stove. "Maybe he just needs a night light."

THUMP!

"Put something over the cage," Papa suggests. "It works for birds."

Nana grabs a towel and covers the cage. She waits a few moments. Silence.

"All right. Good night, Drew and Libby. Good night, Tiny." She disappears into the bedroom and slides the door shut.

RATTLE! RATTLE! THUMP!

"Really, Tiny?" I lift the towel. I can see his bowl is empty. Maybe he just wants more food. "Here, have some more rabbit pellets." I open the door and grab the bowl. But before I can close it, Tiny jumps out. "No! Tiny!" I whisper. "Get back in your cage!"

Tiny is not getting back in the cage. He squeezes under my bunk and refuses to come out. I glance up at Libby. She's hanging halfway out of her bunk, her curly hair dangling down around her ears.

"Now what?" I say.

"He's not thumping, right?"

"We are so dead if they catch him out of his cage!" I grab the bag of rabbit pellets and scoop out a handful. "Come on, Tiny." I reach under the bunk and hold the pellets out to the rabbit. I can't see him in the dark, but I feel his whiskers brush my hand, then his hot breath as he grabs a mouthful and starts munching. "Come on." I move my hand back, let him take another mouthful, and then move it again, let him grab some more, until he crawls out from under the bed and into my lap. "Good rabbit." I give him the last few pellets and then pick him up.

"Come hold the door, Libby."

She does and I manage to squeeze the rabbit back into the cage. I close the door and latch it.

THUMP!

"Tiny!" I groan.

"I have an idea," Libby says. She grabs a handful of rabbit pellets from the bag and then sprinkles them through the cage bars onto the shavings. Tiny immediately starts sniffing around for them and gobbling them up.

"That should keep him busy for a while."

Ah, yes, my sister the mini Einstein.

We cover the cage with the towel and head to bed.

I can hear Tiny shuffling around in his cage, hunting for rabbit pellets. Eventually he stops moving and the trailer goes quiet. Finally!

I close my eyes. It's been a long day. And tomorrow is probably going to be just as busy.

I'm just starting to drift off, when I hear a high-pitched buzzing whine next to my ear, snapping me wide awake. I swat at the mosquito, but in the dark, have no idea where it is or when it's going to land. I lie there and stare at the bottom of Libby's bunk. How am I going to survive six more days of this?

🥕   🥕   🥕

CRASH!

I jump so high, I nearly hit my head on the underside of Libby's bunk. I glance around, for a moment, completely confused as to where I am.

CRASH!

"What in the—" Papa staggers from the bedroom in his pyjamas.

"Is that the rabbit?" Nana says, stumbling after him.

THUMP! THUMP!

Nope. The rabbit is still in his cage. The crashing sound is coming from the bathroom.

CRASH!

I rub my eyes and crawl out of my bunk.

The glowing numbers on the microwave read 5:56. Ugh.

"What is it?" Libby says from her bed. "I'm scared."

Nana goes to comfort Libby. "Papa will take care of it."

Papa opens the bathroom door and pokes his head inside. It's hard to see around him, but from what I can see everything seems normal. No cabinet fallen down. No broken mirror or collapsed shower curtain.

CRASH!

The sound is coming from the roof!

I follow Papa's gaze to the ceiling. The white plastic vent cover is cracked right down the middle and I can see the sky on the other side. Outside, a squirrel is chattering angrily.

CRASH!

"Those filthy little tree rats!" Papa points to the vent. "Look what they've done!"

"What did we do to make them so mad?" I say.

"I'm going to find out." Papa crams his feet into a pair of shoes and heads outside. I follow him into the cool morning air. The sky is cloudy and the sun is barely poking through above the treetops. The clear blue sky of yesterday is gone. I shiver and hug myself.

"Look, Papa!" I say.

The ground around the trailer is littered with large, green pine cones. A squirrel appears on a branch above the trailer, carrying yet another green pine cone. *THUNK!* He drops it on the roof of the trailer, then scampers back into the safety of the trees.

Papa mutters something under his breath, grabs one of the pine cones off the ground and hurls it in the direction the squirrel disappeared. "Stupid animal! Git!"

From the tree branches, the squirrel chatters out a round of angry squirrel insults.

"He's not too happy," I say.

"Neither am I," Papa grumbles. "C'mon, let's go back inside."

7

Just a Little Rain

No sooner do we get back inside than the rain starts. It starts as a *PING! PING!* on the roof, then swiftly turns to a thunderous roar.

"Papa! There's another flood!" Libby cries, pointing at the bathroom. A steady stream of water is pouring through the crack in the vent cover.

Nana runs for the towels. Papa grabs his coat and runs back outside. "C'mon, Drew. Help me with the tarp."

I stand under the awning as Papa rummages through the cubby, finally pulling out a blue tarp and some rope. "We'll need to tie it down so it doesn't slide off or blow away." He climbs the ladder on the back of the trailer, holding the tarp. Between the two of us we manage to cover the vent and tie the tarp down.

Soaked, we head back inside.

Nana passes us each a small hand towel. "Sorry," she says, gesturing to the pile of soggy towels heaped on the bathroom floor. "The rest got wet."

Ugh. "Wait. This one's still dry," I say, pulling the towel off Tiny's cage.

"It's also full of holes," Papa says.

I glance down at the towel. The edges look like Swiss cheese.

Nana sighs. "Well, I guess that belongs to the rabbit now."

I do my best to towel off and then change into some dry clothes.

"At least the rain will keep the squirrels away," Papa says.

"How long do you think it'll last?" Nana says, peering out the kitchen window at the downpour. "Sheila's not going to like this. Kind of hard to hold a pancake breakfast in a monsoon."

Papa chuckles. "She'll make it happen somehow."

While Nana and Papa brew coffee and sit down to watch the morning news on the small built-in television, I feed Tiny a bowl of pellets, scratch him behind the ears the way he likes, and then crawl back into my bunk. Libby's fallen back asleep. I'm not far behind her.

What a morning.

"Drew! Oh, Drew!" Libby's voice pierces my warm cocoon of sleep.

I pull my blanket over my head. "Just five more minutes."

"Come on, Drew! We're having pancake breakfast, remember?"

"Rise and shine, sleepy head." Nana squeezes my foot. "Time to get up."

"So tired." I moan and roll over. "Give me two more minutes."

"No time for that," Papa says. "You've got to get up now."

"One more minute?"

"Up, up, up," Nana says, patting my leg.

"Thirty seconds?"

"*Now*, Drew!"

Ugh.

I roll out of bed and stagger for the bathroom.

"Toilet's broken, remember?" Papa says.

"How could I forget?" I mutter, even though I really did. I turn and stumble back to my bunk, pull out my suitcase, and grab some clean clothes. Then I head back to the bathroom to change.

When I come out, everyone is waiting outside under an extra-large umbrella Papa is holding.

"We aren't going to drive?" I say. The rain has lightened a bit, but it hasn't stopped.

"It's just a little rain!" Papa says.

A little? If the puddles get any bigger, we should think about building an ark.

"What about Tiny?" Libby says. "Shouldn't we bring him?"

"Tiny will be fine. You can take him for a walk after breakfast."

The four of us huddle under the umbrella as we follow the road to the beach. As we pass the outhouses, Papa stops long enough for me to run in and use the bathroom. It's still pretty gag-worthy inside, but at least the rain seems to have got rid of the smell hanging in the air outside.

Libby is splashing in puddles when I come out. She's got her yellow sundress tucked up between her legs like a diaper and is jumping from puddle to puddle in her pink plastic sandals.

"You're going to get wet," Nana says.

"No, I'm not!" she says, just as she lands in a big puddle, splashing water onto Nana, Papa, and me.

Nana sighs. "Let's just get going."

When we get to the fork in the road with the sign that says "Beach Access," we turn onto a gravel trail. It takes us past an empty playground and the log building that holds the laundry and showers. At the end of the trail, we finally reach the beachfront campsites. In the gaps between the trees, I can see the sand stretching out almost to the two islands off the shore. Only a thin line of silvery blue-grey ocean separates them. A lone surfer is carrying his board down the beach. He's dressed in a black wet suit. I think we could all use wet suits at this point.

We turn left and follow the road until we reach the two beachfront sites Sheila has reserved. The smell of bacon and pancakes greets us. So much better than stinky outhouses. I can hear voices, too, talking and laughing.

"Here we are," Papa says, gesturing to a giant shiny motor home parked in the last campsite. It looks like a tour bus a rock star would use. Totally out of place here.

We round the front of the motor home and I stop short. The campsite is almost completely enclosed in a giant screen room attached to the side of the motor home.

"Wow! This is what *we* need, Papa!" I say. No rain. No bugs.

"It would be perfect for Tiny," Libby says.

Papa doesn't say anything. He just harrumphs loudly.

Nana opens the screen. A welcome mat is at the entrance. "Take off your shoes," Nana says to Libby and me, kicking off her sandals next to the pile of shoes already there.

Seems a bit odd, but okay. I take off my flip-flops and sweep my feet on the mat and follow her through the open screen.

Inside, the ground is covered with several large plastic carpets. Around the top, white patio lights have been strung through the poles that make the frame of the room. In the centre hangs a black metal chandelier, lights blazing. At the far end, an outdoor kitchen area is set up, complete with sink, microwave, and fridge. A large camp stove is sizzling with bacon strips, sausages, and fat, fluffy pancakes. Ralph is overseeing it. He's wearing a black apron that says "King of the Grill," holding a flipper at the ready. Next to him is a table with a coffee maker, kettle, and a pitcher of orange juice.

In the middle, there's a group of patio chairs and folding side tables that look more like they belong in a magazine than a campground. A couple of Nana and Papa's friends are seated there, talking. In the centre, there's a fire pit burning. Not the old rusty metal ring that comes with the campsite, but a fancy wrought iron fireplace with carved legs and decorative fake wood. Next to them, a television is mounted to the side of the motor home, playing a golf tournament.

Closest to the entrance, instead of a picnic table, there's a large table with a half-dozen fake wicker chairs around it. It's covered with a fabric tablecloth and has plates and cutlery already set up. A vase of flowers sits in the centre next to a pair of tall candles.

I glance at Libby. Her eyes are round as dinner plates. "This isn't a campsite," she says.

She's got that right!

"Well, hello strangers!" One of Nana and Papa's friends gets up. He's a tall guy with a beard and a Hawaiian shirt.

"Gord! Good to see you!" Papa claps him on the shoulder.

A thin woman with super short brown hair joins him. She's wearing what look like floral pyjamas, only they can't be pyjamas because she's got a silver necklace and bracelets on that jingle when she moves her hands. Unless she wears her jewellery to bed, too.

"Drew, Libby, these are our old friends, Gord and Brenda Nelson," Papa says.

"Great to meet you kids. We've heard so much about you," Gord says, shaking hands with both me and Libby. His smile is contagious and I can't help smiling back at him. "Sheila tells us you've got a rabbit."

"His name is Tiny." Libby beams.

I brace myself for the joke about hunting, cooking, or eating rabbits that I know is coming next. But Gord surprises me by saying, "Well, you should bring him by later. We'd love to meet him."

"We will!" Libby promises.

"It's such a shame Jim and Dot couldn't make it this year," Nana says.

"How is Jim doing?" Papa asks.

"Since his heart surgery, much better," Brenda says. "But his doctor wants him to take it easy."

At that point in the conversation, I completely tune out.

"I see you've finally made it!" Sheila says, coming down the steps out of the motor home, holding a large tray of sliced fruit. Her little dog follows her as far as the top step, then stands there quivering and wagging its tail. It's wearing a pink sweater that says "Mommy's Princess."

Nana takes the tray from her. "We had a bit of a slow morning."

Slow? I hardly call being woken at sunrise by angry squirrels then having to stop a waterfall of rain coming into the bathroom a slow morning!

"Well, you're here now, so we can eat." Sheila picks up Princess and tucks her into her arm, like a baby. "Hungry, kids?"

My stomach growls. Actually, I am.

Ralph brings over a plate heaping with pancakes and places it on the table. "Let's eat!"

Let's eat indeed!

Libby and I grab some plates.

"Now, now," Sheila says. "Manners, please. Wait your turn."

"Aw, let the kids go first," Gord says.

"We can wait." Brenda nods her agreement.

Sheila frowns. "Very well." She turns to me. "Once you've got your food, you two can go sit at the picnic table." She points to the battered wooden table outside the screen room. It's got an umbrella propped over it dripping rainwater onto one of the benches. Great.

Nana helps Libby with her plate and I help myself. On closer inspection of the food, I'm not feeling so hungry anymore. The pancakes are full of seeds, the bacon isn't real bacon, and the sausages seem to be some sort of formed meat alternative. "What is this?" I whisper to Nana.

"Ralph is watching his cholesterol," Nana says, as if that explains everything.

Brenda winks at me. "Try the duck bacon. It's good."

"I, uh, think I'll have some fruit," I say, loading up my plate with chunks of watermelon, pineapple, and strawberries.

"Me, too," Libby says, making a face.

"Now, now." Nana frowns. "At least have a pancake. Ralph makes the best oatmeal chia flax seed pancakes."

Ugh.

With our plates full, Libby and I head to the picnic table outside, while the adults settle around the table and fire pit to eat. I poke at the pancake on my plate. It looks like bird food.

Libby is staring at her plate. "I thought we were having real pancakes," she says.

Yeah, me too.

After everyone has eaten and everything is cleaned up, Sheila announces, "Is everyone ready to go over the schedule of activities for this week? We've got lots planned." She hands out sheets of paper printed with the schedule to the adults. "We've had to make a few changes due to the weather, but we should still be able to get everything covered by the end of the week. A little rain won't discourage us!" Then she proceeds to go over each activity in painstaking detail.

My stomach rumbles. But not from hunger. I need to use the washroom. All that fruit combined with those bird seed pancakes has gone right through me. No way I'm using those outhouses, though. "Hey, um, Sheila?"

"Please don't interrupt, Drew."

"But I need to use the bathroom. Is it okay to use yours?"

"There are bathrooms up by the showers. You can use those, okay?" She gives me one of her persuasive smiles.

"Bathrooms? Like with flush toilets?" I say.

"Of course. And sinks, too," she says, smiling at me like I'm trying her patience.

The other adults chuckle. I don't care. Why didn't anyone tell me this before? I am saved. No more stinky outhouses!

"I gotta go too," Libby says.

"Take your sister," Nana says.

I grab Libby and propel her toward the exit. "C'mon. I gotta go. *Now*."

She doesn't resist. "Me, too." She looks about as uncomfortable as I feel.

I walk-run all the way to the shower house, Libby right on my heels. She hangs a left into the ladies'. I turn right and almost crash into a closed door. A sign hangs there: "Closed for cleaning."

Noooo! This can't be happening! I bang on the door. "Please, I need to use the bathroom now!" No answer. I try the door. It's locked. Seriously?

I'm hopping from one foot to the other, trying to decide whether I should make a break for the outhouses, when Libby comes out of the ladies'.

"Is there anyone in there?"

"No," she says, giving me a confused look.

"Stand guard. Let me know if you see anyone coming."

"You can't use the ladies'!"

"Oh, yes I can!" Didn't stop me going into the girls' change room at school. Of course, that was for other reasons involving revenge and tuna fish. This is an emergency. And there's no Principal Dicastillo to catch me here. I push past her and into the bathroom, run into the nearest stall, and plop down on the toilet. And not a moment too soon.

I'm just finishing up when I hear Libby cough a few times outside. Then I hear voices. Female voices. Oh no!

I pull up my shorts and hurry out of the stall just as two women walk in, dressed in rain ponchos.

They jump back like they're about to be attacked. "What are you doing in the ladies' washroom?" the shorter of the two says.

"The ladies'? What are you doing in the men's bathroom?" I say.

The taller woman points at the female figure on the sign clearly displayed on the open door.

"Oh! Oops!" I say. "I thought this was the men's."

They wait while I wash my hands, and then I hurry out of the bathroom.

"You were supposed to warn me," I mutter at Libby as we head back to the campsite.

"I did. I coughed. Didn't you hear me?"

"Well, yeah, but I didn't know that was a warning! You could've told me before!"

"You didn't give me a chance!"

"Look, next time—"

"No way! Next time you go into the ladies' washroom, I'm telling."

Ugh. Why do little sisters have to be so annoying?

8
Unbelievable!

Nana and Papa meet us on the road.

"Come on, we need to get back to the trailer," Papa says. "We're going on a hike."

"But it's raining!" I protest.

"I hope you two packed rain gear," Nana says.

"Mom packed my rain coat," Libby says helpfully.

"Um," I say. Of course I didn't pack rain gear. It's the middle of July. Rain was the last thing on my mind. "I guess I kind of forgot?"

"We *are* camping in a rainforest," Papa says, frowning.

"I think we've got a spare poncho." Nana pats Papa's arm. "Drew can wear that."

As soon as Papa opens the trailer door, we are met with a loud *THUMP!*

"Poor Tiny," Libby says, going to his cage and opening the door. He sticks his head out and Libby has to push him back inside before he jumps out. "He wants out."

"What about his walk?" I say. "You said after breakfast."

"Sorry, Drew, there just isn't time." Papa shakes his head.

"But he'll be in his cage all day!" Libby's lower lip juts out.

"You can take him for a walk later," Nana says. "And if you're sure he'll use the cage for a litter box instead of the floor, maybe he can come out for a bit when we get back."

That seems to cheer Libby up. She gives Tiny a scratch behind his ears, then a kiss on his nose and closes the cage. She gets her pink and white spotted coat and ladybug umbrella from her suitcase. "Ready!"

Nana hands me the extra poncho and I put it on. It's bright fluorescent yellow and way too big. I look like I'm wearing a giant neon garbage bag. It would even be big on Papa. It drags on the floor, nearly tripping me when I walk.

Nana grabs a pair of scissors. "Let's just fix that." She trims the bottom off the poncho. "Much better."

I want to die of humiliation. I'm just glad none of my friends are here to see me like this.

"All right. Everyone out to the truck." Papa leads the way. "We've got some hiking to do."

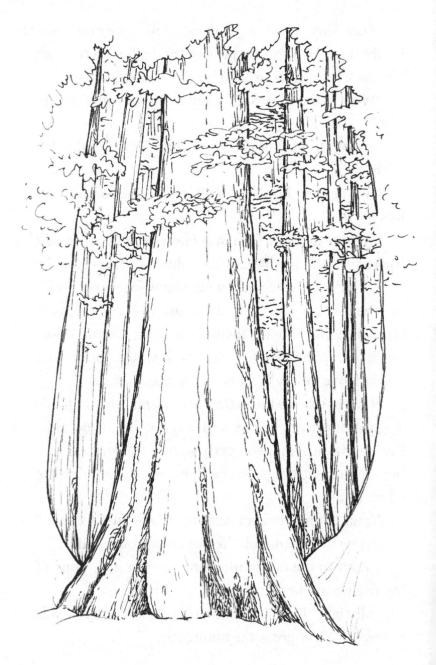

The first part of the hike turns out to be not so bad. We get to see some big trees—some so big you could park a car inside them—and one that's over 800 years old. Nana wants to take our picture in front of the big tree, but I pretend I don't notice and move out of the shot before she can take it. She snaps Libby's picture instead.

The rain is much lighter in the forest, but it somehow feels colder and wetter. The air smells like dirt and a bit like mold. There are lots of interpretive signs along the trail that talk about the forest and the animals and plants that live there and how they depend on each other. We take our time crossing a cool bridge made out of a huge fallen tree. In the ravine below, instead of water, the forest floor is covered with thick ferns and moss.

On another part of the trail, a long wooden staircase climbs up over a tangle of old fallen trees. Sheila has brought her little dog in a pet stroller and she needs the men to help her carry it up and down all the stairs. I can tell it bugs Libby that Princess gets to come, but Tiny doesn't. Actually, it kind of bugs me, too.

"Have you ever seen trees as big as these, Drew?" Gord says, aiming his camera towards the canopy above us.

I think about the big stump in the woods by my house. It's not even near as big as some of these trees. "Only in pictures."

"I think that's true for most people. These trees are some of the last this size on earth. Once they're gone, it'll be hundreds of years before people see trees this big again. Think about that."

I gaze up at them and wonder what it will be like when all the big trees are gone. Then I wonder what it was like hundreds of years ago when there were big trees like this all over Vancouver Island. It must've been so different than today with all the highways and cities everywhere.

At the end of the hike, we climb in the truck and drive further down the highway to the Visitors Centre on Wickaninnish Beach. We meet up with the rest of the group in the parking lot.

"I hope everyone has worked up an appetite," Sheila says. "After we tour the Visitors Centre, we'll be stopping for lunch."

The Visitors Centre is actually pretty cool. There's a hand-carved cedar canoe with First Nations whalers, a long house, and a tree that shows how the salmon feed the forest. Nana wants to take our photo in front of the big whale tail. Since I pulled off my poncho the minute we stepped inside, I let her. We go up to the observation deck, but we don't see any whales or seals or anything. We watch the waves crashing on the beach for a while, then head back downstairs. It's lunchtime and the restaurant is filling up with tourists. A sign out front advertises fish and chips and seafood chowder. My stomach growls. One bird seed pancake and some fruit doesn't hold you over very long.

"I'm hungry," Libby says. I think she ate less than I did. "When do we eat lunch?"

"Right now, if you want," Nana says.

I'm just deciding whether to order a cheeseburger or the fish and chips, when Papa says, "All right, let's head out to the truck."

"The truck? Why don't we just eat here?" I say.

"We already packed a lunch," Nana replies. "The plan was for a picnic on the beach. But the weather doesn't seem to be cooperating."

I glance at the rain streaking down the big windows and the crashing ocean waves, dark grey sky, and the empty beach beyond. Definitely not cooperating.

Ralph and Sheila pass us on the way to the parking lot. Sheila checks her watch. "So we'll meet up again at two o'clock in Ucluelet?"

"Yup. See you then," Papa says.

"Great! We've got so much more to see!" She and Ralph head into the restaurant.

I gaze after them. Bet they'll be ordering the fish and chips.

In the truck, Nana hands Libby and me each a sandwich. I unwrap it and wrinkle my nose. Tuna salad with bits of celery, onion, and pickles. Yuck. I glance at Libby. Her sandwich looks just as gross. She makes a face at me.

"Um, Nana, is there anything else?" I say.

"You don't like tuna? Your mom said you did." She rummages in the cooler at her feet. "There's either egg salad or salmon."

"Do they have celery?" Libby asks.

"Yes, they both do," Nana says. "Don't you like celery?"

"Not really."

"How can you not like celery?" Papa raises his eyebrows at us in the rearview mirror. "I thought you *loved* salad?"

"Well, yeah. Lettuce and cucumber and radishes. But not celery."

Nana hands Libby a napkin. "Here. Pick out the celery and put it on this."

"Hey, Nana, I need a napkin, too," I say.

Nana sighs and hands Libby and me a whole stack of napkins. "Just eat."

I eat as much of the tuna as I can without eating any of the onion or celery or pickles. Which is not easy to do. More than once a piece of onion or celery sneaks in and I have to spit it out. Most of my sandwich ends up in a pile on my napkin. Yuck. I wash it down with a juice box. At least I'm not starving anymore. Just really, really hungry.

After lunch, we drive to the little town of Ucluelet. There's a historic lighthouse there we're supposed to see. Nana puts on the Mini Bops CD again and Libby starts singing along. Only this time I don't have my iPod to drown it out. I stare out the window, willing this day to hurry up and end. The rain has grown heavier, and Papa has to turn the wipers on high speed to keep up with it.

"I think I see hail," I say.

"I think you're right," Nana says, frowning at the ice pellets bouncing off the road ahead of us.

"It'll let up," Papa says. "Just wait and see."

But it doesn't. It's still pouring rain and hailing when we get to the parking lot. And the wind has picked up, too.

"I saw a sign for the Aquarium back there." I point back towards town. "Maybe we could go do that instead of hiking?"

"I want to go to the Aquarium!" Libby says, giving Nana and Papa the same pleading look she gives Mom when she wants cake and candy. "Can we go, please, please, please?"

"We're going another day." Nana puts on the hood of her poncho.

"Do we really have to hike in this weather?" I say.

"This is the west coast, Drew," Papa says, opening the door to a blast of wind and rain. "It rains. Time to get used to it."

I slump in my seat. I will never get used to the rain. Other kids seem to have no trouble being outside when it's wet. But not me. I hate being cold and damp. I'd rather stay inside and play video games or read a comic book.

Unlike the rainforest trail, this trail offers no protection from the rain and wind. It follows the rocky shore line along the edge of the peninsula. Every time the wind blows, it catches the bottom of my poncho and blows it up into my face, soaking me with rain. Ugh. By the time we reach the lighthouse, I'm pretty much wet from head to foot. What was the point of even wearing the stupid thing?

The lighthouse isn't anything like what I expected, either. It looks more like a big white metal box with a smaller white metal box stuck on top of it, and then the light stuck on top of that. Nothing like you see in pictures or on postcards. And there's a parking lot right behind it. We could've driven right up here and skipped the whole stupid hike altogether.

Then Nana wants pictures of Libby and me in front of the lighthouse. Not a chance. I try to duck out of the picture, but trip on my stupid poncho and land face first in a mud puddle. I stand up dripping. Great.

"Let's just get you home and changed." Nana sighs.

We climb into the truck. The second we pull out of the parking lot for home, the rain stops and the sun comes out.

Unbelievable.

9
"Rabbits Are Dumb!"

When we get back to the campsite, I'm cold, I'm wet, and I'm dirty. After a hot shower, I just want to crawl into my pyjamas and into bed.

But Libby has other plans.

"Tiny needs to go for a walk."

I hate to admit she's right, but the rabbit has kicked all the shavings out of his cage and pulled most of the towel through the bars into it—and then peed on it. He grabs the cage door in his teeth and rattles it loudly.

"Poor Tiny," she says, opening the cage to let him out.

"First the two of you need to clean up this mess," Nana says, opening the cupboard and handing me the broom and Libby the dustpan. "This is exactly why he needs to stay in the cage."

"But if we let Tiny out, he wouldn't get bored and make messes!" Libby says.

"We can't trust him to behave when we're not here. He needs to stay in his cage."

"But Nana—!"

"No buts!" Papa says. "Now listen to your grandmother. Clean up this mess and take your rabbit outside."

Libby's lip is jutted out so far she could trip on it.

Libby holds the dustpan and I sweep up the shavings. Then I pull the towel out from between the bars.

"What do I do with this?" I ask Nana.

She sighs. "I'm not washing it. Just throw it out."

I ball up the towel and chuck it in the garbage.

Then I fill the bottom of the cage with clean shavings and refill Tiny's bowls.

When I'm done, Libby has put Tiny's harness back on and attached the leash. "Come on, Tiny, let's go get you some yummy grass." She gives the leash a little tug to get the rabbit to follow her.

"Don't go too far," Nana says, pulling out a package of chicken breasts from the fridge. "Dinner will be ready soon. You do like chicken burgers, I hope?"

"No celery?" Libby asks.

"No celery."

Libby and I nod.

"Okay, outside with you."

"Can we go to the park?" I ask. I want to get as far away as I can from the mosquitos that are sure to be swarming now the rain has stopped. Plus I could use the bathroom. A real bathroom.

Nana glances at Papa.

"Let them go," he says. "I can get them when dinner is ready."

Finally! Some fun!

I grab the rabbit. Libby and I race to the park as fast as our legs will carry us. We're not giving the mosquitos any chance. The dismal grey clouds have broken up into soft white puffs and the sky is a brilliant blue. The sun has dried up most of the rain except for a few puddles in the shadier spots under the trees. Birds are singing and the smell of barbecue wafts in the air.

There are a bunch of kids already at the park play-ing on the playground or riding bikes or throwing a Frisbee when we get there. A couple moms are sitting at a picnic table with a stroller beside them, chatting. The couple with the little dog from yesterday are walk-ing along the road on the far side. I set the rabbit down on the grass. The minute his feet touch the ground he starts gobbling grass like he's tasting it for the very first time in his life.

"Stay here. Don't go anywhere," I tell Libby.

"I won't." Libby bends down and strokes the rabbit's giant ears. "We don't want to go anywhere, do we, Tiny?"

Tiny ignores her and just keeps inhaling grass.

I leave Libby holding his leash and quickly use the washroom. When I come out, she and Tiny are completely surrounded by other kids.

"He's so cute!" a girl about Libby's age coos.

"Does he eat carrots?" one of the bike riders, a boy a year or two younger than me, asks.

"Why is he so big?" an older girl wants to know.

"Can I pet him?" a little boy says.

"Tiny loves carrots," Libby tells the bike rider. "But they're just a treat. Rabbits should eat mostly hay or grass." She turns to the older girl. "He's so big because he's a giant breed. There are other giant breeds like the Checkered Giant and French Lop." Then to the little boy, "Tiny likes to be petted." She shows him how to pet Tiny the way he likes. "His favourite spot is behind the ears." Next she shows them some of the tricks he can do. When she says, "Up!" he stands on his hind legs. When she says, "Spin!" he turns in a circle.

Libby is clearly in her element. She answers all their questions and then some. By the time she's done, I think the other kids know as much about rabbits as I do.

"I want a bunny, too!" the first girl says. "They're so smart!"

"Rabbits are dumb!" a voice sneers.

"Yeah, rabbits are for babies."

I spin around. It's the terrible twins from yesterday—thankfully without their dog. Ugh.

"Rabbits aren't dumb," the older girl says, setting her hands on her hips. "You're dumb."

"Yeah, who asked you?" the other boy with the bike says.

"Get lost, Jake and Logan!" another kid says.

"Just leave us alone," I say.

"Whatever," Jake or Logan—I'm not sure which—says. "Who needs a bunch of babies?"

"Play with your stupid rabbit," his brother adds.

The two stalk off to the playground.

"Ignore them," the older girl says. "They're just jerks."

"You got that right," I say.

"C'mon. Let's play Frisbee."

I glance at Libby. She and the other little girl and boy are sitting cross-legged on the grass, petting Tiny and still talking about rabbits. Although Libby is doing all the talking.

"Sure." I shrug.

"I'm Sam," the girl says with a smile. She has braces with pink and purple elastics on her teeth.

"Drew."

We head out to the middle of the field and start

tossing the Frisbee back and forth. I find out Sam is from Kelowna and her name is actually Samara, not Samantha, and her mom and dad are divorced, and she's here until Sunday, the same day we go home.

The kids with the bikes go back to riding the path around the park. A little while later, the moms collect the little boy and girl and take them away. Then Sam's dad calls her to dinner.

"See you around," she says and takes her Frisbee and goes.

Pretty soon, it's just me, Libby, and the twins left. Uh oh.

"Hey, Libby," I say, trotting over to her. "We should go."

"But Tiny's not done yet."

The rabbit hasn't stopped eating since we got here.

"Well, I think he's gonna have to be. Not unless you want another run in with Jake and Logan."

The twins have also realized it's just us and are heading over from the playground.

"I'm not scared of them." Libby sticks out her chin.

Well, maybe I am. Okay, not so much scared of them, but I would rather avoid another bunch of insults hurled at us.

"Come on. I bet dinner is ready. Maybe Nana made salad."

Libby doesn't move.

"What if they get Moose?"

That gets her going. I grab Tiny and head up the trail.

"Hey, rabbit lovers!" one of the twins yells behind us.

"Where you going with your big dumb rabbit?"

Just then I spot Papa further up the trail coming our way.

"Hey, Papa!" I call and jog towards him.

When we catch up with him, I quickly glance back at the park. But the twins are nowhere to be seen.

🥕 🥕 🥕

"Nana, there's no salad." Libby slumps in her seat at the dining table.

"You're right. I'm sorry. I forgot." Nana says, holding out a bowl to her. "Coleslaw is a kind of salad, too."

"But it's not lettuce salad."

"Tomorrow, I promise."

Libby nibbles her chicken burger but doesn't say anything.

Nana sighs.

I glance at Tiny, back in his cage. He's curled up in the far corner having a nap, one giant ear swivelled in our direction. I don't think he's too upset about the lack of salad. He just ate a truckload of grass at the park.

Me, I'm just grateful for real food. I can't eat my chicken burger fast enough. Plus the coleslaw, baked beans, and corn on the cob Nana made for us. Yum!

"Come on, eat up, Libby." Papa nudges her plate toward her. "After dinner, we're going to Gord and Brenda's campsite to sing karaoke."

Karaoke? Ugh. "Do we have to go?"

"Yes."

"Do we have to sing?"

"Not if you don't want to. But it's more fun if you do."

"Can we bring Tiny?" Libby says. "They said they wanted to meet him."

Nana and Papa exchange glances. "Well ..."

"He'll be good. I promise!" Libby begs. "We can keep him on his leash the whole time."

I shrug. "If he causes any problems we can just bring him back to his cage."

"He better not cause any problems," Nana says. "He better be on his best behaviour."

"Oh, he will!" Libby says, and takes a big bite of her burger.

I glance at the rabbit. His ear turns in my direction and he blinks one eye, as if he's winking at me. I just hope she's right.

10
It's Tiny

ord and Brenda's campsite is next to Ralph and Sheila's. But unlike Ralph and Sheila's, theirs is a *real* campsite. They have one of those giant silver trailers that looks kind of like a spaceship. Colourful patio lights hang from the awning and there's not a single bit of bug screen to be seen—not that you even need any down here by the beach. The breeze off the ocean keeps the bugs away. There are a bunch of folding lawn chairs just waiting to be sat in spread around a real fire pit with a crackling wood fire already started. The picnic table is covered with a checkered tablecloth and bowls of snacks sit on top of it, ready to be sampled.

Nana heads inside to find Brenda, leaving Papa, Libby, me, and Tiny outside.

To the west, the sun is hanging low in the sky, turning the beach and the water beyond it a blazing orange and yellow and red. Some people are walking their dog along the water's edge and further up the beach kids are flying a kite. I wonder if they'd let me join them. It looks like a lot more fun than singing karaoke.

Against the trailer, Gord has just finished setting up a sound system with black speakers and a karaoke machine between them. He spots us and comes over.

"I see you've brought your furry friend," he says to Libby with a big smile.

"This is Tiny," she says proudly.

At the sound of his name, Tiny stands up on his hind legs like he's begging for treats.

"Tiny, huh? With a name like that, I was expecting a much smaller rabbit!"

"Well, he used to be little when we got him," I say. "We didn't know he'd get this big."

"Does that mean he gets bigger?" Gord's eyebrows go up.

"I hope not!" Papa laughs.

"Some Flemish Giants get up to twenty pounds," Libby says. "Tiny is only fourteen."

"*Only*! He's bigger than some dogs!"

Not all dogs. I think about Moose.

About that time, Sheila and Ralph come over from their campsite. Sheila has her little dog tucked into her pink bag again.

Ralph spots Tiny and his eyes narrow. "Keep that thing away from me. I'm allergic."

"Sorry Ralph, we forgot," Papa says. "Should we take him home?"

"Nah," Gord says. "If he sits upwind from him, he should be okay." He points to one of the lawn chairs nearest the beach.

Everyone finds a seat. Nana and Brenda bring out drinks for everyone. The adults get some fancy blended-up drinks with strawberries on the rims. Libby and I get some different fancy drinks with little miniature umbrellas and red maraschino cherries.

"Have you had a Shirley Temple before?" Brenda asks, setting the drinks at the picnic table for Libby and me.

"Uh, no." I eye the glass of yellow and pink liquid. I'm not sure if I want to drink anything that's pink and has a girl's name.

Libby takes a sip. "Oh, it's good, Drew. Try it!"

I taste the drink. It's actually not too bad. But then I think about the kids at the park walking by and seeing me drinking this stuff. "You can have mine, Libby. I'm not thirsty."

Her face lights up at the prospect of two fancy drinks.

"All righty then. Everybody ready for some karaoke?" Gord asks, rubbing his hands together. "Kids? You want to start?"

"Uh ..." I say. "Not really."

"I'll go first!" Libby says, jumping up and nearly spilling her Shirley Temple on me.

I grab the glass before it goes over. "Watch it!"

"Sorry, Drew!"

I take Tiny's leash from her and she runs over to Gord. He shows her how to work the karaoke machine and she picks out a song and starts singing. She doesn't know the words and she can't read fast enough to keep up with the machine, so she just starts making stuff up. I'm not sure if I should be amused or embarrassed for her. The adults all seem to be amused and start clapping along, which just encourages her to sing louder and make up even crazier words.

Oh, yeah. Karaoke is a ton of fun.

When Libby is done with her song, she hands the microphone back to Gord and comes back to the picnic table and her drink.

"All right, Drew. You're up."

"Uh ..." I point at my glass. "Gotta finish my drink first."

"Your drink? I thought you said I could have it!" Libby crosses her arms.

"I, uh, changed my mind?"

"I can make you another," Nana tells Libby.

So that's how I get stuck drinking a yellow and pink Shirley Temple. Ugh. I really hope none of the other kids walk by right about now. Just the thought of them strolling by while I'm sipping away at this girlie drink makes me want to crawl under the table and hide.

Sheila decides it's her turn at the karaoke machine next. She hands her little dog to Ralph and takes the microphone. If I thought Libby was a horrible singer, I was *way* wrong. Sheila sounds like a dying cat. She starts screeching out some slow love song from a gazillion years ago. She must think she sounds good, because she holds the microphone close to her mouth with cupped hands, closes her eyes, and starts swaying back and forth. Ugh.

THUMP!

Clearly Tiny feels the same way I do. I look under the picnic table. He looks plain out terrified. His eyes are bulging, showing the whites, his ears are straight up in the air, and he is so tense his fur is practically vibrating.

"Hey, Tiny. It's okay." I put a hand out to pet him and he jumps away like he's received an electrical shock.

THUMP!

"Aw, don't be scared, Tiny!" Libby says.

THUMP! THUMP!

Papa leans over to me and whispers, "Do you think you could keep him quiet?"

"I'm trying!"

THUMP!

"Try harder!"

I glance at Sheila. I can tell she's annoyed. Every time the rabbit thumps, she wails a little louder. And every time she gets louder ... *THUMP!*

I climb under the picnic table with the rabbit. If I think Sheila sounds bad, I can only imagine how she must sound to someone with giant ears. I pull the rabbit over beside me and try to pet him to calm him down. But he's having none of that. *THUMP!*

"Here. I know." Libby crawls under the table with me. She covers his ears with her hands. I can almost feel him sigh with relief. My sister, as usual, is brilliant. Not that I'd ever tell her that. I just wish we'd brought earmuffs.

Finally Sheila stops her caterwauling and hands off the microphone to someone else.

Tiny seems to have fallen asleep, so I climb out from under the picnic table.

"Hey, Drew." Gord calls me over to him, standing by the door to the trailer.

I go over to see what he wants.

"You want to earn ten bucks?"

"Uh, sure."

He gestures to a bulging white garbage bag sitting next to the steps. "Would you mind running this up to the dumpster?"

Ten bucks for one bag of garbage? If only Mom and Dad paid so well! I don't earn a dime to take out the garbage and recycling at home every week and it's way more than one measly bag.

"Right away!" I say, grabbing the bag.

"Oh, are you heading to the garbage?" Sheila says, getting up from her chair.

"Um, yeah."

"Come with me."

She leads the way over to her campsite. "These could go out, too." She points to four huge black garbage bags sitting next to their RV.

"Uh," I say. "Are you paying?"

"I paid you with breakfast this morning. Now, hurry up. This isn't taking itself out." And she turns and marches back to the party.

Ugh. I stare at the giant pile. How does someone produce that much garbage in one day? Suddenly sipping Shirley Temples and singing karaoke doesn't seem like such a bad thing.

With a sigh, I grab one of the bags and try to lift it. Good grief, what is in this thing? Concrete? I set Gord's bag down and lift the big black bag with both hands. I can barely keep it off the ground. I set it down. There's got to be one that's lighter. I try another bag. Then another. There isn't. They all weigh a ton.

Ugh. I need to find a better way to do this. I glance

around. Something to put it in and push it to the dumpster would be perfect. Something like a wagon or a cart or—my gaze falls on the perfect solution—a *pet stroller*.

I grab the stroller, figure out how to unfold it, and then wrestle the first giant bag of garbage into it. I give it a trial push. It wobbles a bit, but rolls with no problem. This is going to be *so* much easier!

Since Sheila probably isn't going to think too much of me borrowing her precious Princess's stroller for garbage duty, I take the long way to the park instead of the more direct route past Gord and Brenda's site and Sheila's prying eyes. I find the dumpster behind the laundry. With a bit of struggling, I haul the heavy bag out and heave it into the dumpster. I hear an angry chitter come from inside. What the—? A big, fat raccoon jumps out, gives me an annoyed look, and then scuttles away.

"Sorry about that!" I call after it.

It doesn't answer.

I shrug and head back for bag number two.

Without too much trouble, I dump bags two and three. Bag four isn't so cooperative. It's the heaviest of them all and as I'm lifting it into the stroller—*RRRIIIIIPPP!*—the bag tears and some garbage splats out onto the ground. A drizzle of gross-smelling liquid trickles onto Princess's stroller, making a puddle in the bottom. Ugh.

Quick as I can, I glance around for something to clean it up. I spot a white tea towel folded on the table. I grab it and wipe up the mess. But now I've got a dirty tea towel. I glance around trying to figure out what to do with that. I throw it into the sink and turn on the water. No water comes out, though. I look underneath and find a water shutoff valve and turn it. Water sprays out of the faucet and all over the place. Including me. Ugh. Ugh. Ugh.

I rinse out the towel until its mostly white again, then refold it and lay it on the table. Then I find a broom and dustpan and clean up the spilled garbage, sticking it back into the hole in the bag. Then I wrangle the bag—hole side up—into the stroller and hurry to the dumpster. I throw it in and race back for Gord's white kitchen bag. As I round the last corner before the campsite, the stroller starts wobbling like crazy and suddenly the back wheel falls right off. Oh no! This can't be happening!

I grab the wheel and try to reattach it. Fortunately, it pops back on without too much trouble. It's still pretty wobbly, but at least it's reattached. I push the stroller back to the campsite at a much slower pace.

When I get there, I fold it up and put it back where I found it, then I grab the last bag, Gord's white kitchen bag, and take it to the dumpster. I use the bathroom— might as well since I'm here—wash my hands and head back to the campsite for some more karaoke.

Sheila is going back onstage. "This one's for you, Ralphie." She blows her husband a kiss, then closes her eyes and starts wailing away at another prehistoric love song. Yuck.

Gord spots me and hands me a crisp ten-dollar bill. "Thanks, Drew."

"No problem," I mumble and stuff it into my wallet.

I plop down at the picnic table. Libby is working on her third Shirley Temple. She's got cherry stems lined up on the table like trophies. "Nana gave me two cherries this time," she says.

I peek under the picnic table. Tiny's poor ears must be aching again. But Tiny's not there. The leash dangles from Libby's wrist, but there's no rabbit attached to it. It's been chewed in half!

"Uh, Libby," I say. "Where's Tiny?"

"He's under—" She glances under the picnic table and her eyes grow huge. "Tiny? Tiny! Where are you, Tiny?"

We jump up and start searching the campsite. No Tiny by the fire. No Tiny under any of the adults' chairs. No Tiny anywhere.

"What's going on, kids?" Papa says.

"It's Tiny!" Libby says, holding up the chewed leash.

"*ACHOO!*" Just then, Ralph lets out a gigantic sneeze.

97

My gaze snaps over in his direction. "I think we've found him!"

"*ACHOO! ACHOO! ACHOO!*"

I'm about to race over to Ralph, when a flicker of movement by the trailer catches my attention. Tiny! He is no longer downwind from Ralph, he's very much upwind. He's all the way across the campsite, sniffing around the karaoke machine. Before I can say or do anything, he reaches over with his mouth and chomps the cord to the microphone, silencing Sheila. Her screeching stops mid-wail. Then, with a flick of his hind feet, the rabbit squeezes under the trailer and disappears.

11
Troublesome Rabbit

This is why he needs to stay in the cage," Nana says as we walk home.

I want to say, "No, this is why the rabbit needs *out* of the cage!" At home, Tiny has the run of our whole house and he causes way less trouble than he has in two days here at the campground. He needs "exercise and mental stimulation," as Libby's favourite book, *The Ultimate House Rabbit Guide Book,* says. But I don't say that. I'm too tired to argue with her.

We just spent the last twenty minutes trying to coax Tiny out from under the trailer. He seemed to think it was good fun hopping around under there, just out of our reach. The adults armed themselves with brooms, umbrellas, and even the crank for the trailer's awning and tried chasing him out with those, but he'd always dodge them at the last second and go back to sitting in the very centre of the trailer. I think the only reason he came out was because he got bored.

Libby has a full pout on right now. "Just get a banana!" she kept telling them. "He'll come out if you get a banana." But no one would listen. Least of all Sheila. Like she knows anything about rabbits. She could've just stopped barking orders at everyone and Libby and I could've coaxed Tiny out in a few minutes. But no. She had to do it her way. Now everyone thinks he's a dumb troublesome rabbit. I feel a bit like pouting myself.

At least I didn't have to pay back the ten dollars like Sheila wanted me to. "It's his rabbit. He should have to pay for the damage."

But Gord refused to take it. "No need for that. It's just a microphone cord." Then in a lowered voice to me, he added, with a wink, "Between you and me, I'm not much of a karaoke fan, anyway."

Well, that makes two of us.

When we get back to the trailer, Nana has us put Tiny in his cage and then sends both Libby and me to bed, even though it isn't fully dark yet.

Nana and Papa go into their bedroom and shut the door without another word.

I lie in bed and stare at the bottom of Libby's bunk. Can this day get any worse?

THUMP!

I groan. Of course it can.

🥕 🥕 🥕

It's raining again when we wake up in the morning. Big surprise. I can hear the rain pinging off the roof before I even open my eyes.

"Come on, you two. It's time to get up." Nana makes a lot of noise in the kitchen, banging pots and slamming cupboards.

I bury my head under the covers. We're supposed to go to the Botanical Gardens and the art gallery today. If I didn't know this was planned ahead of time, I'd think Sheila was torturing us for spoiling her karaoke yesterday.

Tiny rattles the cage bars.

"Your rabbit wants his food." Nana says "rabbit" like it's a bad word.

I climb out of bed, give Tiny a scoop of pellets and a nose rub, then head for the bathroom.

"Toilet's still broken," Papa says from the dining table, his face hidden behind the pages of *Golf Digest*.

"Still?"

He sets the magazine down. "I looked at it yesterday. We'll need to get some parts when we're in town today."

Ugh. I get dressed and head to the outhouses.

The Botanical Gardens are just as boring as I expected. Wandering around in the rain wearing that enormous neon yellow poncho looking at plants and weird art is not my idea of fun. About the only thing interesting there are the chickens. But, of course, Sheila doesn't let us look at them for longer than a few minutes. Libby seems to like it, though. When we stop at the cedar-shingled hut overlooking the reedy frog pond, she leans over and whispers, "What if there were fairies here, Drew?" Ugh.

At lunch, Sheila complains because she had to cancel the reservations at the local brewery because of us kids. She didn't have to. She and the other adults could've gone for lunch and I'd happily go back to the campground with Libby. Instead, we get stuck having a picnic in the truck again. At least this time Nana has left out the celery from our sandwiches.

After lunch, we drive into Tofino to go to the art gallery. Actually, it's art galleries. Plural. How many art galleries can you squeeze into such a tiny town? And how many paintings and carvings and sculptures can you look at before you die of boredom?

Worst of all, as we're searching for a parking spot on the street, I catch sight of a skate park in the Village

Green. A skate park. Okay, sure, it's raining and it's not like skateboarding in the rain is much fun, either. But given a choice between that and trooping from art gallery to art gallery, I think it's pretty obvious which I'd pick.

Finally, after what seems like hours, Sheila tells us we've got free time—as if we're on a school field trip. "You can explore the town or do some shopping or head back to the campground if you choose." She checks her watch. "We'll meet up again after dinner at the campsite." Then she dismisses us. Like students.

"Does this mean we can go home now?" I say.

"Just as soon as we pick up a few things for dinner," Nana says and takes Libby and heads towards the grocery store.

"We can't forget salad!" Libby says as they walk away.

"It's at the top of my list." Nana pats Libby on the hand.

"Come on, Drew." Papa heads for the hardware store. I follow behind him.

While the man helps Papa at the counter, I wander around the aisles.

In the camping aisle, I run into Sam and her dad looking at the tent repair kits.

"Oh, hi, Drew!" she says, with a big smile.

"Uh, hey, Sam."

"Our tent got a hole in it," she says. "The mosquitos can get in."

"That's lame. A squirrel broke the vent in our bathroom. We had to cover it with a tarp."

Sam laughs. "I wondered why your trailer had a big tarp on it."

"Yeah, the first morning. Rain poured inside. Papa wasn't very happy."

"Oh, wow. Yeah, I don't doubt it!" She grins, showing her braces.

"All right," Sam's dad says, standing up with a patch kit in his hands. "I think this will do it. Coming, Sam?"

"Coming." She starts to walk away, then turns back towards me. "See you later, Drew?"

"Sure thing," I say and smile at her.

"Great!" She smiles back and hurries off after her father.

"There you are!" Papa says, appearing at the end of the aisle where Sam and her dad just were. "It's time to go."

I trot over to his side. "Did you get the parts you need to fix the toilet?"

"No. They've got to order them in. Should be here tomorrow, though."

No toilet till tomorrow? Ugh.

We get Libby and Nana and the groceries and head back to the Wind & Tide Beach Resort and Campground. Once again, the rain lets up the second we leave town. I'm beginning to think we should talk to Sheila about rescheduling all her activities for after four o'clock in the afternoon.

When we reach the campsite, we park the truck, grab the groceries, and head into the trailer. At the top of the steps, Nana stops. "Why is the rabbit out of its cage?"

Huh? I peek around her. Tiny is stretched out on the couch, head on his front paws, fast asleep. On the floor, his cage door is standing wide open.

I glance at Libby, but if she knows anything she's not letting on.

"Did you make sure the door was latched after you fed him this morning?" Papa asks me.

"I think so." I try to remember, but I was half-asleep at the time. Maybe I forgot to latch it. But I don't think so.

"Well, get him back in his cage." Nana sighs. "I just hope he hasn't ruined anything important."

I climb into the trailer, grab the rabbit, and stick him back into his cage, a.k.a. jail cell. He's not too impressed with the idea. And I don't blame him. He's had full run of the trailer all day. *THUMP!*

"Aw, don't be sad, Tiny!" Libby says, digging through one of the grocery bags and pulling out a head of green leaf lettuce and a bundle of parsley. "Look what we got you!"

"I bought that for dinner!" Nana says. "You said you wanted salad!"

"We can share with Tiny," Libby says. "Can't we, Nana?"

Nana crosses her arms. "He can have what's left after we eat."

"But he's hungry now!"

"Then give him more rabbit food. His bowl is empty."

"Please, Nana! He needs fresh vegetables, too."

I nod my agreement. "At home, Mom gives him a big salad every day."

Nana sighs. "One leaf."

"And some parsley?"

"Okay. Some parsley, too."

Libby tears off a leaf of lettuce and a few stems of parsley and sticks them through the bars for Tiny. He gobbles up the parsley like he's slurping up spaghetti. Then he starts mowing through the lettuce leaf.

Nana and Papa are doing a close inspection of the trailer, looking for anything he's chewed or peed on. Aside from Papa's issue of *Golf Digest*, which he'd left sitting on the couch this morning and is now shredded to bits, there doesn't seem to be anything else Tiny has wrecked. Until Nana walks into her bedroom and shrieks.

We all rush to the door. In the middle of the floral comforter is a large orange puddle.

"I thought you said he was housebroken?" she exclaims.

"He is," I say. "At home he never pees on anything." Tiny used to pee on my bed every day—sometimes more than once—but that hasn't happened in months. Not since I started being nice to him.

"I think he's mad that he has to stay in his cage," Libby says.

"Well, peeing on beds isn't the way to get what he wants." Nana yanks the sheets off the bed and heads for the laundry, muttering to herself about how she goes on vacation to get *away* from doing laundry.

"Well," Papa says when she's gone. "I think I'll get some shuteye. Why don't you take your rabbit to the park? You can come back with Nana when she's finished the laundry."

Libby likes this idea. She gets Tiny out, puts him in his harness, and attaches the leash. It's a lot shorter now because we've had to tie a knot in the middle where Tiny chewed through it. Now I wish I'd thought to ask about getting him a new one when we were in town earlier.

I pick up the rabbit and we head to the park. Tiny seems very interested in where we're going, and keeps trying to climb up my shoulder for a better view. I scratch him between the ears and he nibbles my hair.

"You let him out, didn't you?" I say to Libby, as we walk along.

"No-o!" Libby says. "I think *you* left the cage open."

"Libby, I didn't leave the cage open. You can't let the rabbit out when we're not there. He could've really wrecked something. Or hurt himself. You don't want him to hurt himself, do you?"

"No." She pouts. "But it's not fair he has to stay in the cage all the time."

"I don't think it's fair, either. But we have to do what Nana and Papa say."

Libby doesn't say anything, just keeps trudging toward the park, her lower lip sticking out.

"Just promise me you won't let Tiny out again."

"I didn't let him out," she says. "So I'm not promising anything."

Ugh.

12
BANG! BANG! BANG! BANG!

The kids at the park spot Tiny the second we get there and come crowding around to pet him and ask Libby more questions.

"I have a velociraptor," the little boy from yesterday says, showing Libby his plastic dinosaur. "Rawr!"

Tiny bumps his nose against the toy and then rubs his chin on its head and goes back to gobbling up grass.

I don't see Sam amongst the faces, but I see two faces I know I don't want to see. Jake and Logan are lurking around the playground, casting dirty looks in our direction.

I ignore them. What is their problem anyway? Does it matter so much that we have a rabbit and brought it camping?

The boys with the bikes are racing along the trail

that circles the park. I wish I'd thought to bring my bike. It's still bungeed to the back of the trailer.

"Hey, Libby," I say. "I want to get my bike. Don't go anywhere, okay?"

"Okay." She doesn't even look up. She and another little girl are making daisy chains with dandelions. At least she's trying to. Every time she adds a flower to the top of the chain, Tiny eats one off the end. "Tiny!" she says, pretending to be annoyed. She feeds him another dandelion.

"All right. Be right back," I say and race back to the campsite, arriving out of breath and panting. I go around the back of the trailer and unhook the bungee cords from my bike. Of course, I don't think about what order I'm unhooking them, and before I can unhook the last cord, my bike falls to the ground with a loud *CRASH!*

Great. I pick it up and make sure I haven't broken anything. It's got a scratch on the front fork. The brand new front fork I finally saved up enough from my paper route to replace. I let out a loud sigh, then go grab my helmet from the trailer. Papa is still snoring away, so I tiptoe in and tiptoe out so I don't disturb him.

I clip on my helmet, grab my bike, and fly back to the park.

Libby hasn't moved. No surprise. She's finished her dandelion daisy chain and has it looped around her neck. She's working on another. Probably for Tiny.

The boys with the bikes spot me and zoom over. "Hey, wanna race?"

I grin. Of course I do!

We race around the park a few times. I come in second twice and third the last time, but I don't mind. It just feels great to be on my bike again. I'll beat them next time for sure.

Some of the moms show up at the park then and call their kids to dinner. "Gotta go!" The boys on the bikes wave and ride off.

I'm just riding back towards Libby when I spot trouble. There's a big rotten stump not far from where Libby and her little friend are sitting, and I spy the twins crouching behind it.

"Hey!" I yell just as the twins high-five each other and run off, laughing.

I pump the pedals faster. What are they up to?

Suddenly there's the loud *BANG! BANG! BANG! BANG!* of firecrackers from behind the tree.

The girls scream and Tiny flattens himself to the ground like he's being swooped down on by an eagle. Then he bolts. The leash is yanked right out of Libby's hand and the rabbit takes off into the woods. Oh no!

Libby screams again. "Tiny! No! Stop! Tiny!"

The twins, now back at the playground, are laughing like they've just seen the funniest thing ever.

Libby starts to cry. "You guys are jerks!"

I don't bother with them, though. I race after the rabbit on my bike. I can see the white underside of his tail flashing ahead of me as he tears through the woods at high speed. I pedal as fast as I can through the ferns and bushes, dodging trees and stumps. He races through a campsite, startling the family eating dinner there.

"Sorry!" I yell, as I pedal through after him.

He runs through a couple more campsites, causing shouts of surprise and alarm, before charging back into the woods again.

"Tiny!" I yell, even though I know it's not going to do any good. "Tiny, slow down!"

At last he stops by a fallen log and flops onto the ground, breathing hard. I can still see the whites of his eyes flashing and his nose is flaring red from running. I get off my bike and put my foot on the end of the leash before he can run off again. He doesn't move. I grab the leash and stroke his head. "Poor bunny. Those kids are mean."

I look around. We aren't too far from the road, but now I have a problem. How do I get both the rabbit and my bike back to the park?

I tie Tiny's leash to a tree, then push my bike up to the road. I realize our campsite is just up the road. So I quickly push my bike over to it and dump it by the picnic table. Then I run back to the woods to find Tiny. He's right where I left him by the fallen log. I untie the leash, scoop him up, and head back to the park.

When I get there, Libby isn't anywhere to be found. Great. I check the laundry. Nana's not there, either. I check the ladies' washroom, but there's no one in there. A girl gives me an odd look as she walks past me and into the bathroom. "This is the ladies'," she says.

"Uh, yeah, I know. I'm looking for my sister."

"Well, she's not here." She lets the door swing shut in my face.

I hurry back to the campsite. Nana is waiting by the

picnic table, arms crossed. Libby is with her. Her eyes are red from crying.

"This is no way to treat your bike, Drew," Nana says.

"Sorry," I mumble, setting the rabbit down to pick up the bike. "I had to get Tiny."

"Tiny!" Libby cries, running over to hug the rabbit. She buries her face in his caramel-coloured fur. "Don't you ever run away again. I was so scared."

"Maybe the park isn't the best place for him," Nana says.

"But he has to eat grass!" Libby protests.

"He can eat grass somewhere else!" Nana says.

"It was those twins!" I say. "Jake and Logan, they're the problem!"

"So Libby tells me. I think it's time your grandfather had a word with their parents. Where is their camp-site?"

"I don't know," I say.

"Well, I think it's also time we found that out." Nana turns to go into the trailer. "Until then, the rabbit needs to stay here."

After dinner, Papa drags me all over the camp-ground, searching for the twins' campsite. There are 175 campsites at the Wind & Tide Beach Resort and

Campground. So this takes some time. We've wandered up and down every road in the campground at least twice, I'm sure, when I finally spot Moose, tied to a long clothesline between two trees.

"That's Moose." I point to the dog.

Papa leads the way to the campsite. A pop-up tent trailer and a small dome tent occupy the site along with a bunch of beach toys, bikes, and other camping gear piled up between them. A man is sitting in a lawn chair by the fire, sipping from a can in a foam holder that says "Keep Calm and Drink On." A woman is washing dishes in a plastic tub on the picnic table.

The second we get close to the campsite, Moose starts barking his head off.

"Shut up, Moose!" the man yells.

Moose doesn't shut up, but keeps barking. The neighbours must love him.

"Moose!" the man yells again. "Go lie down!"

This time the dog obeys him, going to lie down as close to the trailer as his chain will let him, but not before getting in one or two last barks.

About that time, the man and woman spot us.

"Afternoon," Papa says with a friendly smile, walking up to stand beside the picnic table. "Nice weather we're having."

The man grunts a greeting. "What can I do for you?"

"Are you Jake and Logan's father?" Papa says.

"They're not here right now." He waves a hand at me. "They've gone down to the park."

"We were wondering if we could have a word with you about them."

"What have they done now?" The woman dries her hands and crosses her arms. She has the same dark hair and freckles the twins do.

"Never mind, Angie." The man gets up. "I'll deal with this." He comes over to where Papa is standing. He's a big guy. Tall and thick, like a tree trunk. He sets his hands on his hips and looms over Papa. "What seems to be the problem?"

Papa doesn't seem intimidated by him. He looks the man in the eye as he speaks. "My grandson here, Drew, and his sister were at the park with their pet rabbit and it seems your sons got up to a bit of mischief with some firecrackers. Scared the bunny pretty good."

"A rabbit? You brought a rabbit camping?" The man guffaws.

"Tiny likes camping," I say. He really *does* seem to like it. Being stuck in a cage all day and all night, not so much. But being outside—either in the woods or at the park—he seems to be as much at home as he is at home.

"Well, maybe camping isn't the best place to take a rabbit." The man takes a swig of his drink. "Too many dogs around."

"We'll keep that in mind for the future. But he's here now," Papa says. "All we're asking is for you to have a word with your kids and ask them to leave the rabbit alone. He's not doing them any harm."

"You telling me how to raise my kids?"

"Not at all." Papa raises his hands. "I'm just asking you to be considerate of your fellow campers."

The man stiffens and his eyes narrow. "And you call coming around here telling me what I should do with my kids being considerate?"

"I'm sure they didn't mean it." The woman comes to stand beside her husband. "They were just having fun."

"Oh, I'm sure they didn't, either." Papa gives her a smile. "But we'd sure appreciate it if you could ask them to not trouble with the rabbit anymore."

"And we'd sure appreciate it," the man says, "if you wouldn't stick your nose in other people's business."

"Not my business?" Papa says. "I'll have you know that if your children's behaviour is affecting my grandchildren then it is *very* much my business. In fact, it may very well be the campground's business. I'm sure they would *love* to hear your children were setting off firecrackers unsupervised on their property. And that your dog was threatening to attack another guest's pet. I'd really hate to see your camping trip cut short."

The man doesn't reply. He just stands there scowling at Papa. His wife doesn't look much happier.

"Now, if you please, keep your children—and your dog—away from my grandchildren. Good day to you." With that, Papa turns and propels me out of their campsite.

As we walk back down the road to ours, Papa says, "If you see those kids again, Drew, I want you to avoid them, okay?"

I nod my head. He doesn't need to worry. That's exactly what I intend to do.

13

Fun and Games

When we get back to the campsite, Nana and Libby are waiting for us at the picnic table, both wearing long sleeves and wrapped in beach towels. A Tupperware tray of baked goods is sitting on the tabletop between them.

"How did it go?" Nana says, swatting away a swarm of mosquitos and getting up.

Papa shakes his head. "I don't know if they got the message, but I said my piece."

Nana sighs. "I guess that's it then. The rabbit is just going to have to stay here at the campsite."

"But he needs to eat grass!" Libby says. "He can't just eat pellets. He'll get fat. And his teeth will grow too long."

"One week without grass won't hurt him," Papa says.

"You don't know that," Libby says, her lower lip sticking out.

"Libby!" Nana says. "Enough. The rabbit was supposed to stay home. Your grandfather and I are doing our best to accommodate him, but he just isn't going to have full run of the trailer and the campground like he does your house. Now come along, we're late for Games Night."

"Games Night!?" Papa says. "Oh, lordy. I plum forgot."

"Can't we do something fun instead?" I say. "Like go to the beach and have a campfire. You promised us s'mores, remember?"

Nana frowns at her wristwatch. "Maybe, later. We were supposed to be there half an hour ago. Now come along. Sheila isn't going to be happy."

She's got that right. When we get to the campsite, Sheila's lips are pursed so tight it looks like she swallowed a lemon. Two actually. And a jar of pickle juice to top it off.

"We had to start without you. You'll need to wait until the next game." She pulls a card from her hand and slaps it down on the pile on the table.

"Sorry we're late," Nana says. "I've brought some date squares."

Sheila nods toward the folding table next to the grill. It's already spread with more desserts than the eight of us could eat in a week. My mouth waters as

Nana unwraps her date squares and sets them next to a plate of Nanaimo bars and a box of cookies. I'm just deciding which I'll start with—the Nanaimo bars, some cookies, or maybe a lemon tart—when Sheila swoops in between me and the dessert table.

"You may each have *one* dessert," she says, looking first me, then Libby, square in the eye until we nod with agreement. "Then take it out to the picnic table. I don't want mucky fingerprints everywhere."

As if we're both five.

I decide to choose a piece of chocolate cake instead of a Nanaimo bar, just because it's the biggest dessert there. Libby takes a lemon tart and we go out to the picnic table. Sheila follows behind us and plops a giant stack of napkins on the table beside us. "No sticky fingers," she says, like we've already forgotten what she said ten seconds ago.

She marches back to the games' table with the other adults, leaving Libby and me with our treats.

I carve a wedge of cake with my fork and lift it to my mouth. This is going to taste so good. But instead of gooey chocolatey goodness, I just about gag. Coffee! It tastes like burnt coffee! Yuck. I spit the cake out on my plate and stare at it misery.

Libby has nibbled the pastry edges from her lemon tart and is licking the whipped cream off the top. "Want a taste, Drew?" she says. "It's so yummy."

"It's okay." I sigh. I poke the cake with my fork and it topples over. Ugh.

Inside the bug screen tent, the adults are setting up a new card game, laughing and talking loudly. Gord says something and Papa howls with laughter and claps him on the shoulder. It must've been pretty funny, because even Ralph is laughing. Nana and Brenda are serving more drinks, though no fancy drinks for us kids. Sheila comes down the RV steps, carrying a stack of board games. Her little Chihuahua watches her from the top step, shivering, as she marches over to us.

"If you weren't going to eat it, then why did you take it?" Sheila says, setting the board games on the picnic table and stabbing a finger at the half-eaten cake in front of me.

"I didn't know it tasted like coffee," I mumble.

"Then you should've asked." She grabs the plate.

"Sorry," I say.

"Are your hands clean?" she says. "Hold them up."

I hold up my hands for her to inspect. Libby does the same. Sheila checks them over and seems satisfied they're not dirty.

"Well, I hope you like board games. This is all I've got for kids. Make sure you don't lose any pieces. Some of these games I've had since I was about your age." She turns and marches back to the screen room and the other adults.

I watch her go, wondering if it's possible Sheila was ever our age. As she goes through the screen door, a moth flutters into the bug zapper hanging above it. *BZZZT!* It goes up in a puff of smoke. Right now I feel about the same as that moth.

"Look, Drew! Look! Candy Land!" Libby pulls an ancient-looking box from the stack. Sheila was definitely right. The games are old. Some of them look like they've been sitting in a dusty attic for the last fifty years. "Can we play it? Pleeaaase?" Libby pleads, clasping her hands together and holding them out in front of her.

Ugh. "No way. That game is for babies."

"Then what about Cootie? I get to be the pink bug."

"Not on your life." I study the stack of games. Yahtzee. Boring. Uno. Too many rules. Libby would never keep up. Mystery Date. It's pink and got girls on the cover. Not even touching that. "What about Operation? That's fun, right?"

"Okay!" Libby nods.

I pull the game from the stack and we get to work setting it up.

First problem: half the pieces seem to be missing.

Second problem: dead batteries.

When I open the battery compartment, the batteries look like they've melted in nuclear waste. "Yuck."

I put the game back in the box. Though really it should go straight into the garbage.

Libby looks disappointed for a moment, then her face lights up. "Wait! They've got Scrabble! We can play Bananagrams!" She pulls the box out and dumps the wooden tiles onto the picnic table with a clatter. "Help me flip them all face down, Drew."

"You can play Bananagrams with Scrabble?" I say.

"Yup!" She nods like a bobble head. "Ms. Lee told us last year if we don't have Bananagrams at home, we can use Scrabble letters instead."

"Cool." I start flipping letters.

We're just about done, when Sheila comes storming over. "What are you doing? Didn't I say to be careful not to lose any pieces?"

"We're not losing pieces," Libby says. "We're playing Bananagrams! It's fun!"

"Banana what?"

"Bananagrams," I say. "It's like Scrabble, but you don't need a board to play."

"It doesn't matter," Sheila snaps. "You have to play the games the way they're supposed to be played, or you're not going to play them at all. Now clean that up. If you can't follow the rules, then you can sit on your hands."

Libby looks stunned, like she's just been slapped in the face. Then she quietly starts putting the tiles back into the box. But I can see the tears starting to form in her eyes.

"We weren't going to lose any pieces," I mutter under my breath.

"What was that, young man?"

Nana gets up from the adults' table and hurries over. "Now, now," she says. "Is there something else they can do, Sheila?"

Sheila sniffs. "Well, I've got some crayons and colouring books. But I was saving those for another night."

Crayons and colouring books? Seriously? She really has no clue.

"Can't we walk down to the beach?" I say. There are a bunch of people there, walking their dogs, running, sitting on beach chairs. A few are still playing in the water, even though the sun is hanging so low in the sky it looks like it's going to drop right into the ocean.

"You can't go down to the beach unsupervised, Drew." Nana shakes her head. "We'll go to the beach another day.

I sigh. "Come on, Libby, let's play Candy Land."

Libby wipes her nose and gives me a smile. "No thanks, Drew. I want to colour now."

Of course she does.

Sheila brings out the colouring books and crayons and the adults go back to their card game. I grab a colouring book and flip it open. There's a teddy bear sitting on a potty. There's a teddy bear washing its hands.

Another is counting out squares of toilet paper. "Remember to wipe!" it says at the bottom of the page. A colouring book on potty training? Where's that coffee cake so I can choke on it?

After one game of cards with the adults, Nana and Papa decide it's time to head back to the trailer. Nana claims she's tired and us kids need to get to bed early.

I groan. Bedtime? It's hardly even dark yet. Of course, given the alternative—sitting here with crayons colouring teddy bears and toilets—going to bed doesn't sound so bad after all.

"Don't forget your date squares," Sheila says. If her lips pinched together any tighter, she'd swallow them.

I make sure I use the men's room on the way back, so I won't have to use the outhouses later. I'm not even close to tired yet. I yawn. Okay, maybe a little, but there's no way I'll be able to sleep while it's still so bright out. I wish my iPod wasn't dead or I'd play some games to keep me busy until I was ready to sleep. Too bad I didn't bring any comic books. I bet the newest issue of *Galactic Bounty Hunter* is out. I'll have to ask Nana and Papa if there's a bookstore or comic shop around here.

When we get back to the campsite and troop into the trailer, we discover Tiny sitting on the couch, grooming himself. He sits up as we enter, his giant ears swivelling toward us like satellite dishes, then he hops down to greet us.

"Tiny! What are you doing out?" I scoop up the rabbit. He nose-bumps my cheek. I think he's in a much better mood for having been out of his cage so much today.

Nana goes straight to their bedroom to check for pee. There's none this time. Instead, Tiny has pooped all over the bed. Nana sighs and grabs the broom and dustpan. She sweeps the poop off the bed, then strips the cover from the comforter.

"The two of you need to be sure his cage is closed before we go out," Papa says with a stern frown at both of us.

"Yes, Papa," Libby says.

I scowl at her.

She just shrugs. "I was sure I closed the cage, Drew."

Ugh.

While Libby and I put Tiny back into his cage, Papa heads off to the camp store and comes back with a wheelbarrow full of wood. "Ready to roast marshmallows, kids?" he says.

"But I thought we were going to bed?" I gape at him.

"In half an hour." Nana winks at me.

"Unless you'd rather go now?" Papa says.

"No way!" I grin. Finally! Real camping!

Libby jumps up and down and claps her hands. "Yay! S'mores!"

"A promise is a promise." Nana smiles.

While Papa lights the fire, we get out the lawn chairs and beach towels and Nana lights a bunch of yellow candles on the picnic table. With all the rain, the mosquitos have practically tripled in number. I swat at a swarm hovering over my head. I think the candles are like signal fires, letting them know we're here.

We bring Tiny out and after he sniffs around the campsite a bit, he flops down under Libby's lawn chair and takes a nap.

Once the fire gets going, Papa hands us each a long metal skewer. We stab marshmallows onto the prongs and hold them over the flames. Papa shows us how to melt the marshmallows over the coals so they don't burn.

Libby keeps catching hers on fire. But she doesn't seem to care. Nana helps her slide the marshmallow between graham crackers, then squish them together so it melts the piece of Cadbury's chocolate inside. Yum!

I lose count of how many s'mores I eat. But by the time Nana and Papa tell us it's time for bed, I'm stuffed and couldn't eat another bite.

"Now, go wash up and brush your teeth," Nana says.

"Thanks, Nana! Thanks, Papa!" Libby gives Nana a hug and a Papa gooey kiss on the cheek.

Papa waggles his eyebrows at her.

I say thanks, too, then grab the rabbit and carry him inside. He's not too pleased about going back into his cage, but then I give him a scoop of pellets and he seems to forgive me.

I get into my pyjamas, brush my teeth, and climb into my bunk.

For the first time on this trip, I'm actually happy.

14

The Early Worm Catches the Bird

Instead of rain drumming on the roof, I wake up the next morning to the sound of birds singing and a ray of sunlight streaming onto my pillow. I roll over and peek out the small window next to my bunk. For the first morning since we've got here, the sky is actually blue and there's not a cloud in it. Perfect beach weather. But somehow I don't think that's on Sheila's schedule.

"Time to get up, kids," Nana calls from the kitchen.

"The day's a-wasting," Papa adds.

I climb out of bed and glance at the clock on the microwave. 7:15.

"It's barely morning," I say. "I thought we were on vacation."

"The early worm catches the bird!" Papa says with a grin, pouring himself some coffee.

"Don't you mean, 'the early bird catches the worm'?"
I say.

"Not today! We're going birdwatching."

"Birdwatching? Why can't we go to the beach?"

"Let's go to the beach!" Libby pokes her head over the edge of the top bunk. "I want to make a sandcastle! Can we bring Tiny, too?"

"Now, now," Nana says. "There'll be time for the beach later."

"But later it'll probably rain," I grumble.

"Drew, please don't argue. We've paid good money to go on a birdwatching tour this morning. It'll be fun. You'll see."

Fun? Sitting still for hours waiting for birds to show up, just so you can look at them or maybe take their picture, doesn't sound like a whole lot of fun to me. I flop back on my bed and let out a loud groan. "I don't feel so good."

"What's wrong?" Nana asks.

"I feel sick to my stomach. And my head aches."

"Get the Buckley's, Nana," Libby says.

"The what?"

"The Buckley's cough medicine. That's what Mom does if we get sick. It seems to work really good on Drew. Sometimes he doesn't even have to take it and he feels better."

I groan again. Why does Libby always have to wreck

everything? "I really don't feel good," I say and clutch my stomach.

"Well, I don't have any Buckley's. Let me get the thermometer." Nana goes into the bathroom and comes out with an old glass thermometer. She sticks it in my mouth. "Don't bite down on it."

I nod and groan again.

"Come on, Drew," Papa says, patting my leg. "It's just a little birdwatching. And later we're going to the Aquarium."

"Promise?" It's hard to talk with the thermometer in my mouth so it sounds more like "pwom-ith."

"Yes, after lunch. We're all going."

"Yay! I want to go to the Aquarium!" Libby says, climbing out of her bunk and running to get dressed.

Nana checks the thermometer. "You don't seem to have a fever. Maybe some breakfast will make you feel better."

"Yeah, maybe." I sit up. "We're really going to the Aquarium?"

"Yes, Drew."

"Y'know, I think I feel a little better now."

Before we leave, I give Tiny a scoop of pellets and check that his cage door is firmly closed. Then I make sure I'm the last one out, so Libby can't unlatch it before we go.

We're just getting into the truck, when Libby says, "Wait! I forgot something!"

"What?" Nana checks her watch. "We're going to be late."

"Um, just my, um, umbrella. In case it rains."

I look out the truck window. There are no more clouds in the sky than there were when I woke up. "Libby, it's not going to rain."

"It might."

"You don't need your umbrella," Nana says. "Now buckle up, it's time to go."

"Come on, worms! Let's go catch some birds!" Papa says and we pull away from the campsite.

🥕   🥕   🥕

Not surprisingly, birdwatching is just as boring as I expect it to be. Plus it's hot. If it was cold and wet the last few days, today it's like a switch has been flipped and we're now out on the mudflats in a baking hot oven.

"Look over here, everyone," our guide says. "A great blue heron has caught himself a fish."

Papa holds the binoculars for Libby to look through. "Do you see him?"

"He looks just like the ones at home."

Papa chuckles. "Probably. There are lots of blue herons on the island. You want a look, Drew?"

"I'm good," I mumble.

Actually, I'm not good. I'm starting to feel really sick. My head is beginning to spin and my stomach feels really queasy. A cold sweat breaks out all over me.

"Nana," I say, tugging her sleeve. "I don't feel so good."

"Again, Drew?" She frowns at me. "Can't you even *try* to enjoy yourself?"

"No, really, Nana. I feel sick."

"He does look a little green around the gills," Papa says.

"Get the Buckley's!" Libby says.

"Would some water help?" Brenda offers me a water bottle.

I take a sip and hand it back, shaking my head. That just made it worse.

About that time Sheila gets involved. "You are not sick," she says. "I've seen sick. And you are not it."

I groan. I feel like I'm going to barf. "Can I please just go back to the truck?"

"You need to stop making trouble all the time." Sheila wags a finger in my face. "I've put a lot of time and effort into planning this trip and you seem to be determined to spoil—"

Too late. I *am* going to barf. And it's going to be all over Sheila. I try to stop it. I cover my mouth with both hands, but all that does is cause the puke to shoot through my fingers and all over Sheila's face and chest.

She shrieks and jumps back, but not before the rest of my breakfast ends up all over her shoes.

"Oh, Drew," Nana says.

"Gross!" Libby says.

"We better take him home," Papa says.

Sheila, for once, is too stunned to say anything at all.

That pretty much puts an end to our birdwatching tour. Sheila storms off to her car, with Ralph trailing behind dabbing puke off her with a balled-up Kleenex. Gord and Brenda decide, with everyone else leaving, they've seen enough blue herons and sandpipers for one day. And Nana and Papa drag me and Libby to the truck and drive back to the campground. I barf two more times on the trip, but I manage to give Papa lots of notice so he can pull over in time.

When we get back to the trailer, I crawl straight into bed, clothes and all.

Nana heads to the camp store and brings back some Gravol and ginger ale. I manage a few sips of ginger ale to wash down the Gravol tablet. Then Nana and Papa take Libby to the park and leave me to rest. In a few minutes, I'm fast asleep.

I wake up to a furry face and whiskers tickling my nose. I open my eyes and blink a couple times to focus them. Tiny is on the bed beside me, sniffing me all over. He nibbles my hair and then licks me on one eyebrow.

I pull my hand out from under the covers and rub his head. "Libby let you out, didn't she? You better not have peed on Nana and Papa's bed again."

He sniffs around the bed a little more, then flops down beside me so I can pet him. He grinds his teeth with pleasure when I rub his ears. It's called tooth-purring. Rabbits do it when they're happy, and Tiny does it a lot.

I roll over and notice my queasiness is completely gone. I just feel really tired, even though I've been sleeping for who knows how long.

I'm debating whether I should try getting up when Nana and Papa and Libby get back.

"Oh, Drew, you missed the Aquarium!" Libby says. "It was so much fun. They let you pet starfish and sea cucumbers and stuff. You would've had so much fun!"

"The Aquarium?" I sit up. "What time is it?"

"Almost five," Nana says. "You were still fast asleep when it was time to go, so we thought we'd just let you keep on sleeping."

"We left you a note," Papa says, pointing to a notepad on the dining table.

136

Ugh. I flop back on my pillow. I was really looking forward to going to the Aquarium.

"I see you let the rabbit out," Nana says, going to check their bedroom. "He better have behaved himself."

Luckily he has. There's no pee *or* poop on Nana and Papa's bed.

"Feeling better now?" Papa says, coming to sit next to me on the bunk.

"Actually, yes. A lot better."

"Great! Because we're going to a show tonight."

"A show? Like a movie?"

"Something like that. It's called Journey into the Rainforest."

"Uh, sounds, um, great."

"It'll be fun, Drew," Libby says. "They have puppets and stuff."

I force a smile. "Can't be worse than birdwatching, right?"

"As long as you don't go throwing up on anyone else." Papa chuckles.

My face burns. "Yeah, about that. I'm really sorry."

"That's all right, Drew." Papa ruffles my hair. "I guess we should've believed you."

"How's Sheila?" I ask.

"She's fine. Nothing a shower couldn't fix. Though it would probably be wise to be on your best behaviour tonight."

"First let's get some dinner," Nana says. "Do you want soda crackers or toast, Drew?"

I shrug. "Toast, I guess."

While Nana makes dinner, I get up and go to the bathroom and have a shower. I come out feeling pretty much normal. I have no idea what made me so sick, but it seems to have gone away as quickly as it came.

"Did you get the part for the toilet, Papa?" I ask when I come out.

"Not yet, I'm afraid." He shakes his head. "Hopefully tomorrow."

Tomorrow? Ugh.

We eat dinner and I feel well enough to eat not only the toast, but also some of the barbecued salmon and potatoes everyone else is having.

After dinner, Libby wants to take Tiny for a walk. "Please? We won't take him to the park," she promises.

"There's grass by the front gate," I suggest. "We could take him there. I doubt we'll run into the twins."

"Are you sure you're feeling well enough, Drew?" Nana says.

"Yeah, I feel totally fine now." I shrug.

"Well, don't be too long. The show is at eight."

15
CHOMP!

We put Tiny in his harness and race up the road to the front entrance of the campground. There's a big parking lot here for guests as well as the camp office and camp store. Colourful wind socks hang from the awnings of both buildings, fluttering in the afternoon breeze. Large planters on either side of the front doors spill over with flowers. A sign on the camp store says, "Ice Cream Sold Here!" Underneath it, another promises "Fresh Bait!" Several wheelbarrows full of wood are lined up out front. The couple with the pug-nosed dog come out the door, which has been propped open with a painted wooden bear holding a welcome sign. They nod at us as they pass.

"How's Rabbitzilla today?" the man asks.

"Hungry!" Libby grins at him.

Across the parking lot, underneath the Wind & Tide Resort and Campground sign, is a large patch of grass. I carry Tiny over to it and plop him down on the ground. He sniffs around for a second, before finding a tasty dandelion and chomping it up.

I sit on the grass beside Libby with Tiny between us. Libby sets to work building a daisy chain from dandelions. For a while, I watch people coming and going from the store. Within minutes, I'm bored. I wish I had my iPod. Then I could play Mega Velocity while I wait for Tiny to fill up on grass. I lie back on the ground and stare at the clear blue sky. Not even a single cloud to imagine is a shark or a dragon or an alien battleship.

"Oh, hey, you guys," a familiar voice says.

I shield my eyes and sit up. Sam is walking toward us. She's got a purple Popsicle in one hand. With the other, she pulls a pair of white earbuds from her ears and tucks them into her pocket.

"Sam!" Libby says.

"You have an iPod?" I say, probably a little too excitedly.

"iPhone, actually." She holds it up. It's in a white case with funny little black doodles all over it.

"Cool," I say. "Do you have a charger for it?"

"Well, yeah." She laughs. "But not with me. It's back at the campsite. Why?"

"I, uh, forgot mine." I stammer, suddenly feeling stupid.

"Oh, that's lame. Well, you can totally borrow mine. C'mon. We'll go get it."

"Drew, we're supposed to stay here," Libby says. "Remember?"

"It will only take a minute," I say, getting up. "We'll come right back."

"No! We have to stay here. What about Moose?"

"He's probably tied up at his campsite," I say.

"It's no big deal." Sam shrugs, taking a bite of her Popsicle. "I can run and get it and be right back."

She could. But then I'd still be stuck here with nothing to do except wait on Tiny to fill up on grass.

"What if I bought you a Popsicle, Libby?" I pull out my wallet. "I could buy you any colour you want. Maybe they've got a treat for Tiny, too."

I can see the wheels turning in her head as she considers my offer.

I give her an encouraging smile. "A Popsicle *and* some candy?"

"*And* ice cream." Libby crosses her arms.

"You can't have a Popsicle and ice cream at the same time! They'll melt!"

"Then I'm not leaving."

"Fine." I throw my hands up in the air. "You can have a Popsicle *and* some ice cream *and* some candy."

"No."

"What do you mean, 'no'?"

"No, I changed my mind. I won't do it. We have to stay here. I don't want Tiny to get hurt."

"But you just said—Libby!"

Her lower lip is jutting out further and further as I speak.

"Look, if you don't come with us, then I'm going to tell Nana and Papa about the broken toilet."

"You wouldn't!"

"Just try me."

"Fine. But if we see Jake and Logan or Moose, I'm telling."

"Okay by me. Now come on." I grab Tiny, who seems disappointed to be torn away from all the tasty grass, and start towards the parking lot.

Libby doesn't move.

"Now what?"

"You still have to buy me a Popsicle and ice cream and candy."

Ugh. Why do little sisters always have to be such a pain in the behind?

"All right, already. Just come on."

The grin on Libby's face is so big, her cheeks look like they hurt.

I don't know how she does it, but somehow, between the store and Sam's campsite, Libby manages to eat the blueberry bubble gum ice cream cone in her right hand and the pink Popsicle in her left hand—and all without them melting all over her. Besides a smudge of blue ice cream she licks off her chin, she doesn't have a speck of anything on her anywhere. I was sure she was going to end up a pink and blue sticky mess that I'd have to somehow explain to Nana. I can just see how that would go:

"Ice cream? What ice cream?"

"Why would I buy Libby ice cream?"

"No, it wasn't to bribe her! Why would I bribe her?"

Yup, that would go over really well, I'm sure.

While Libby gobbles up her treats, I take my time savouring my double scoop of Moose Tracks ice cream. I'm just munching on the last bites of the cone when we arrive at Sam's campsite.

Her dad's busy chopping kindling with a small hatchet next to the fire pit. He glances up as we approach. "Hey, kids. What's up?"

"I just need to get my phone charger, Daddy," Sam says, going over and unzipping the tent. She kicks off her flip-flops and crawls inside. A second later she comes back out with a white charger cable looped in her hand.

I can't believe it. I am saved. No more dead iPod.

I can play games. I can take pictures and video. I can even read books if I want.

"Here it is," Sam says, handing me the charger.

My heart sinks. This is the wrong charger. My iPod has the fat connector. This one has the skinny one. Ugh.

"What's wrong?" Sam asks.

"Wrong charger." I sigh, handing it back to her. "Thanks anyway."

"Aw, sorry about that."

I force a smile onto my face. "It's okay. I'll figure something else out."

"You can't be the only person here with an iPod," she says. "Somebody else at this campground has to have a charger that'll work for you. I know! Let's go from campsite to campsite and ask."

She can't be serious. I think I'd die of embarrassment. Talk about awkward. *"Hi, you don't know me, but can I borrow your iPod charger?"* Um, no.

"Maybe another time. Libby and I need to get back. I guess we're going to a show tonight."

"At the Green Point Campground Theatre?" Sam's eyes light up. "We're going tonight, too. I've heard it's kind of fun."

Well, that makes me feel a lot better. "Cool. Maybe we can sit together?" I say.

She smiles. "Sure thing."

"Great! See you tonight!" I say.

"Yup! See you!"

We leave Sam and head back to our campsite. My arms are getting sore from packing Tiny around everywhere, so I set him down.

"This way, Tiny," Libby says. "Let's go home!"

The rabbit seems to know which way to go and starts off at a fast run. We chase along behind him—me hanging onto the leash, Libby skipping along next to me.

Then it happens. We round a corner and there are the twins. And Moose.

Before I can say or do anything, Moose goes crazy barking his head off, lunging at the end of his leash—and the twins let him go. He comes charging towards us, snapping and growling. Tiny freezes, his giant ears swivelling towards the dog. Then, with a loud *THUMP!* he takes off running so fast the leash snaps apart where we'd tied it together. Both rabbit and dog go charging into the woods at full speed.

Libby screams. The twins double over laughing. I stand there gaping. It all seems to be happening in slow motion.

"Tiny!" It sounds like someone else's voice, but I know it's mine. "Tiny!"

I find my legs and chase after the rabbit and the dog. I can barely keep them in sight, they're moving so fast. My heart is hammering in my chest. I'm so scared the

dog is going to get to the rabbit before I can. I push past trees and branches, jump a fallen log, and land in mud. I lose my left flip-flop but keep going.

Ahead of me, the rabbit launches out of the woods and heads for the nearest cover, a picnic table. The dog is hot on his heels, still barking its head off. I reach the edge of the woods just as Tiny ducks under the table and the dog goes in after him. I brace myself for the terrible rabbit scream I know is coming, but instead I hear a loud grunt and then an even louder *YELP!* Moose comes scrambling out from under the picnic table and retreats past me, his ears back, his tail stuck between his legs, a trickle of blood running from the end of his nose.

I race to the table. Tiny is crouched underneath, his ears pinned back, his eyes wild. "Tiny," I say. "Hey, Tiny, it's okay." Poor guy. He looks terrified.

Libby comes running up then, tears streaming down her face. "Tiny! Tiny!"

"He's okay," I say, reaching under the table to stroke the rabbit. He flinches away at first, then seems to realize it's me and lets me pet him. "Come on, Tiny," I say gently. "Come on out. Let's go home." I pull on his harness, and he hops out from under the table.

Libby practically smothers him. "Tiny! I'm so glad you're okay."

"Well, he won't be okay if you suffocate him!"

Libby lets the rabbit go. He shivers from nose to tail

and then finds a weed poking through the gravel, snips it off with his teeth and munches it up.

"What happened to Moose?" Libby says.

"I think Tiny chomped him."

Libby starts to laugh and cry at the same time. "Oh, Tiny. You silly, brave rabbit."

"Come on," I say. "We should head back."

I scoop Tiny up and head back through the woods to the road, Libby trailing behind me—only stopping long enough to rescue my flip-flop from the mud.

The twins are waiting there. But no Moose.

"Where's our dog?" the one on the left says.

"Yeah, what did you do with Moose?"

"We didn't do anything with your dog," I say. "He ran off." I point behind me. "That way."

"You have to help us find him."

"What? Why?"

"Because he ran off chasing *your* rabbit."

"Maybe you shouldn't have let him go," Libby says, crossing her arms.

"Moose!" the twin on the left calls. "Moose! Here, boy!"

"Hey, Moose!" the other joins him.

"Well, good luck with that," I say. "C'mon, Libby, let's go."

We leave the twins and carry on down the road. We've just reached the trail that leads to the park, when a big black SUV comes roaring up. I jump back and yank Libby out of the way as it speeds past us. I can see Moose in the back seat, his big white head sticking out the open window, his tongue lolling out.

As soon as it disappears around the bend, I hear the SUV screech to a stop and a door slam. Then yelling. Oh, man, those twins are in trouble now.

16
"Tiny!"

Shhh!" Papa says as Libby and I clatter into the trailer. He nods toward the closed bedroom door. "Nana's not feeling too well."

Uh oh. "Did she throw up?" I ask.

"No, but it looks like she has the same stomach flu you did, Drew."

"Oh." I feel bad. I didn't know I was going to make anybody else sick. Sheila is doomed.

"Are we still going to the show?" Libby asks.

Papa checks his watch. "Yup, and we should get going soon or we're going to be late."

He folds up his tattered *Golf Digest* magazine and sets it on the table. How he can read it with so many holes chewed into it is a mystery.

"Better put Tiny in his cage," he says.

I let Libby get Tiny settled and head to the bathroom to change. I've got mud on my shirt from carrying Tiny. I check the mirror. Better wash my face and brush my hair, too.

Papa looks me up and down when I come out. "Well, look at you all spit and polished. What's the occasion?"

"Uh, nothing."

"Drew's got a girlfriend!" Libby says.

"Do *not*."

"A girlfriend?" Papa's bushy eyebrows go up. "What's her name?"

"Sam!" Libby says.

"Libby!" I glare at her.

"Sam, eh?" Papa chuckles.

"She's not my girlfriend. She's just a girl I met at the park."

"We believe you." Papa winks at Libby.

Ugh.

We climb into the truck and drive to the Green Point Campground in the Pacific Rim National Park. The theatre is a large cedar building painted with First Nations artwork.

I spot Sam and her dad outside.

"There's Sam!" Libby says really loud.

"Hey," Sam says, and comes over to stand with us.

Her dad and Papa shake hands and introduce themselves.

Sam is grinning at me in a strange way. Suddenly, I feel all awkward and don't know what to say.

"Shall we go find our seats?" Papa says.

"Um, yeah," I say. "Good idea."

We troop into the theatre and find a place to sit. There are long benches in rows, some with striped cushions on top of them, sloping down towards the stage. I slide onto a bench next to Sam. She flashes me a smile.

"Excited?" she says. "I am."

"Um, sure."

The lights dim and the show starts. Sam was right, it is actually kind of fun. The presenters are really funny and they talk about some really interesting stuff about the rainforest. Some of it I already know from Science class. And some of it I learned on our nature hike the first day we were here. But I don't care because they make it fun. They play videos and music. They tell stories and sing. We clap along and stomp our feet and laugh a lot.

I glance at Sam at one point and she gives me this really goofy grin. Then she reaches down and takes my hand, lacing her fingers through mine. My heartbeat speeds up to a million miles an hour. I break into a cold sweat. I don't know what to do. My hand feels like it's on fire. Electric shocks are shooting up my arm and into my shoulder. I swallow hard and slowly ease my hand from hers and then wipe it on my shorts. I don't look at her as I do it, just keep looking at the stage, even though I've totally lost track of what's going on. I hear the audience laugh, so I laugh, too. I'm sure she's looking at me, but I won't look at her. My heart just keeps thudding in my chest. My stomach feels queasy and for a moment I'm afraid I'm going to barf again. Thankfully, it passes.

At last, the show ends and the lights come up. I sneak a peek at Sam. She grins at me and says, "That was a lot of fun, wasn't it?"

I somehow manage to make my tongue work. "Oh, yeah. Real fun."

I want to crawl under the bench we're sitting on and die.

The trailer is quiet and dark when we get back. The sun is already down and the sky is changing from gold and red to a deep blue. I can see Venus sparkling above the treetops as we climb out of the truck and head inside.

Papa flicks on the light above the kitchen sink.

"Tiny!" Libby cries. "Where's Tiny?"

My gaze goes to his cage. It's empty, the door wide open. I glance around the trailer. No Tiny on the couch, no Tiny on the bunks, no Tiny under the table, no Tiny anywhere.

"He's got to be here," Papa says, checking the bathroom. No rabbit.

I get down on all fours and looks under my bed. No rabbit.

We check the kitchen cupboards, the pantry, even the fridge. No rabbit.

"Where could he be?" Libby wails.

Papa slides open the bedroom door. "How you feeling, Liz?" he says.

"Horrible." The miserable reply comes from the bed.

"I don't suppose the rabbit is in here?"

"Why would the rabbit be in here?"

"No reason." Papa quietly shuts the door.

Libby plops down on the couch. "I locked the cage. I know I locked the cage." Big fat tears dribble from her eyes and down her cheeks.

Papa sits beside her. "We'll find him, sweetie. He's got to be here somewhere."

"But where? He's not here anywhere! He must've got outside!"

"He's smart, but he can't open doors," I say. "No opposable thumbs."

Papa shakes his head. "No, she's right. He's not inside, so he must be outside. It's the only logical answer." Papa gets up and pulls two flashlights from the drawer in the kitchen and hands one to me. "C'mon. He's got to be around somewhere."

We search the campsite. No Tiny under the picnic table, no Tiny under the trailer, no Tiny under any of the lawn chairs.

I shine my flashlight into the woods and shiver at the thought of Tiny out there all alone.

"Tiny!" Libby calls. "Tiny!"

"Tiny!" I yell louder. "C'mere, Tiny!"

Papa shushes us. "It's getting a bit late for hollering." He takes Libby's hand. "Come with me."

We walk to the next campsite. A family is sitting around their campfire roasting marshmallows just like we were yesterday.

"Evening," Papa says. "I don't suppose you've seen a rabbit?"

"A caramel-coloured one with big ears," I add, holding my hands apart about the length of Tiny's ears.

"Sorry, no. Haven't seen a rabbit like that."

At the next campsite a young guy is waxing down his surfboard.

"A rabbit?" he says. "We saw one in the field earlier."

"A big orange one?" I ask hopefully.

"Nope. This one was little and brown. Probably a cottontail."

We walk up and down the road asking at every campsite. But no one has seen Tiny. Finally, when trailer lights start to wink out and campfires are being doused for the night, Papa calls it quits. "Sorry, kids. We'll just have to keep looking in the morning. Maybe he'll find his way back by then."

"But there's bears, and coyotes, and eagles." Libby sobs. "We have to find him."

"We'll find him, Libby. Keep your chin up." Papa picks her up. "But it will have to wait for morning."

Libby cries the whole way back to the trailer. I feel a bit like crying, too. Tiny may be smart and brave, but these are the woods. He doesn't stand a chance out here.

Papa has us get into our pyjamas and brush our teeth and get into bed.

"We'll find him," he assures Libby, giving her a hug. "In the morning. You'll see."

I hope he's right.

Eventually, Libby cries herself to sleep. I feel so bad for her. If she'd just kept the cage door closed Tiny would still be here. Though it's a complete mystery how he got out of the trailer. It had to have been through the door. There isn't any other way out. Not unless he learned to fly out the broken vent in the bathroom. I get up and check it, just to be sure. But it's pretty clear no rabbit could get out that way. A couple times, I think I hear scratching outside and I get up to peek out the kitchen window with a flashlight. A raccoon waddles across our picnic table, searching for leftovers, but no rabbit.

I hear Papa get up a few times, too. In the darkness, I can just make out his shape staring out the window. I can tell he's as concerned about Tiny as we are.

At last, I can't keep my eyes open anymore, and I fall asleep.

It's barely light when Libby wakes me up. "Drew, we have to find Tiny."

As if I've forgotten.

I squint at the clock on the microwave. It reads 5:45. Way too early. I groan and roll out of bed. The bedroom door is still closed. "What about Nana and Papa?"

"We'll leave a note."

We get dressed, scribble a message on the notepad on the table, and hurry outside into the cool morning air. It's so quiet that, besides a few birds twittering in the forest around us, I can hear the waves breaking all the way down at the beach.

I study the ground around the trailer. Then I walk all around the edge of the campsite, inspecting the soft dirt there.

"What are you doing, Drew?"

"Looking for footprints."

"Oh." Libby copies me, going to the opposite side of the campsite to look.

"Just watch you don't mess up any evidence," I say.

"You're not a detective, Drew."

She's got that right. I can't find a single clue where Tiny could've gone.

"I just don't get it," I say. "We've been here long enough, if Tiny wandered off, he should find his way back. He knows where his home is."

"You don't think," Libby's voice hushes, "someone took him, do you?"

"I don't know what to think, Libby." I shake my head. "I just can't figure how he got out of the trailer. And then why he would just disappear."

"Maybe he went to the park," Libby says. "There's no grass here. Maybe he went there to find some grass and got so busy eating he forgot to come home?"

"Maybe," I say. "I guess there's only one way to find out."

We run to the park. It's completely quiet and empty. No kids, no adults, no dogs. And no rabbit in the field, gobbling grass. We check around the shower house and the laundry, look under the dumpster. No rabbit anywhere.

"Got any other ideas?" I ask.

"Would he go to the front gate?"

I shrug. "All we can do is try."

We head for the front gate, stopping to ask about Tiny at any campsites where people are awake. But no one has seen him.

The lawn under the sign is empty. No rabbit.

I'm really beginning to lose hope.

A campground worker is watering the planters by the camp store with a hose.

"You kids need any help?"

"We're looking for our rabbit," Libby says.

"A rabbit, you say." He pushes his ball cap back to scratch his head. "If you're looking for rabbits, there's a place just up the road that has rabbits."

"No, *our* rabbit," I say. "He's lost."

"Oh, well, can't help you. Haven't seen a rabbit."

I sigh.

Where, oh where, could Tiny be?

17
Clues

We head back to the campsite feeling utterly defeated. I really do feel like crying. Then I get angry. Angry at Libby for bringing Tiny with us. Angry at Libby for leaving his cage open. Angry at Nana and Papa for keeping him in such a small cage. Angry at the twins. Angry at Sam. Angry at myself.

"Why couldn't you just keep his cage closed?" I demand.

"I did, Drew. I promise I did. I locked it last night before we went to the show."

"Then how did he get out?"

"I don't know!" Libby's eyes fill up with tears again.

I sigh and put my arm around her. Neither do I.

Nana and Papa are both up when we get back. Nana looks pale and tired, but she's out of bed and eating toast at the dining table with Papa.

"No luck, huh?" Papa says.

I think it's pretty obvious from our faces how the search is going.

"Why don't you have some breakfast?" Nana says. "Then Papa can give you a hand."

"I'm not really hungry," I say.

"Me either," Libby adds.

"At least have a glass of juice," Nana says, pouring a glass of orange juice for each of us.

We have no choice but to sit down and drink it. I decide maybe some toast wouldn't be such a bad thing and spread a piece with peanut butter and take a bite.

Just then the cell phone in Nana's purse rings. Actually, it doesn't ring, it plays "It's a Small World" over and over. Really loud.

Papa gets up and answers it.

"I'm terribly sorry, Sheila, we're going to have to cancel—"

"Cancel!?" Sheila's voice yells so loud Papa has to hold the phone away from his ear. "What do you mean cancel? You do realize they gave us a special group rate, don't you?"

"Yes, well, Liz has come down with the stomach flu—"

"That doesn't mean you and the children can't come!"

"I'm afraid we won't be coming either. The rabbit got out and—"

"I thought you said the rabbit wasn't going to interfere with my schedule?"

"I'm really sorry, Sheila. But you'll just have to go
without us. We need to find him."

Sheila huffs and puffs a bit more, but finally lets
Papa go. He flips the phone closed and puts it back into
Nana's purse.

"Where were we going?" I ask out of curiosity.

"On a whale-watching cruise," Nana says. "Then on
a hike to Hot Springs Cove."

"Oh." I actually would've liked that.

There's a knock at the trailer door.

Libby launches herself from the table. "Maybe it's
Tiny!"

"Tiny can't knock!" I say.

"Maybe someone found him, dummy!" She runs to
open the door. Papa gets up and follows her.

The same campground worker we saw this morning
is there.

"Did you find our bunny?" Libby says.

"Sorry, kid, still haven't seen a bunny. I'm here to
let you know there's a beachfront site available this
morning if you want it. The current occupants will be
out by eleven."

"Thanks for letting us know. We'll be ready to move
then," Papa says and shuts the door. He smiles at me
and Nana. "Finally some good news."

"We can't move the trailer, Papa!" Libby says. "What if Tiny comes back and we're gone?"

"We'll find him before we need to move," Nana says. "Eleven o'clock is still hours away."

Papa helps us search for Tiny for a while, then decides he and Nana need to get the trailer ready to move. So Libby and I are back on our own hunting for Tiny.

One of the boys with bikes pedals up to us on the road. "Hey, where's your bunny?"

"Lost," Libby says and looks like she might burst into tears again.

"What? Oh no! Can we help look for him?"

"That would be great," I say. "It's such a big campground. He could be anywhere."

Another boy pedals up. "Can I help, too?"

Pretty soon we've got half the kids in the campground searching the woods, checking under trailers and cars, and asking every adult within earshot if they've seen the rabbit. Shouts of "Tiny!" can be heard up and down the road.

"Now we'll find him for sure," I tell Libby.

Sam finds us checking the trail between the outhouses and our trailer for the third time today. My face burns with heat when I see her.

"Can I, um, talk to you privately?" she says, glancing at Libby.

Privately? My face burns hotter and hotter. I don't want to go anywhere privately with Sam. She might want to hold hands again—or worse, try to kiss me. I shudder at the thought.

"Um, it's okay. You can say whatever it is you have to say in front of Libby."

Sam glances awkwardly at Libby. "Well, okay." She takes a deep breath. "I did a lot of thinking last night. I just want you to tell me the truth. Do you want to be my boyfriend or not?"

I want to crawl under the closest rock. Maybe private would've been a better choice. "Y'know, on second thought, how about we go talk over here by the outhouses?" I say.

"I was right!" Libby says. "She *is* your girlfriend!"

Ugh.

I steer Sam over to the outhouses. It's as stinky as ever over here, but better than having this talk in front of Libby. As soon as we're out of sight, though, I get all tongue-tied again. Sam stands there, looking about as awkward as I feel. Finally, she says, "So? Do you?"

I don't want to hurt her feelings, but I sure don't want to be somebody's boyfriend. "Uh, sorry, Sam," I say. "I, uh, can't we just be friends?"

Her brow wrinkles as she considers my words. "You don't want me to be your girlfriend?"

I shake my head no and brace myself for the tears or the angry words or the cold shoulder I'm sure are coming next.

Instead, a look of relief comes over her face. "Oh, thank goodness! I thought you wanted to be boyfriend–girlfriend, but I just want to be friends, too!"

A smile spreads across my face as she speaks. What a relief! I almost give her a hug, then stop myself. That's probably boyfriend/girlfriend territory and I'm not going near that again!

"Are you kissing?" Libby says from the other side of the outhouse.

"No!" Sam and I say at the same time. Then we laugh.

"Come on," I say. "Let's get out of here. It stinks."

The three of us head back up the trail to the road.

"I heard about Tiny," Sam says. "I'm really sorry."

"We'll find him," I say. It's become like a chant I keep repeating over and over in my head. We'll find him. We'll find him. I can't let myself think of any other possibility.

We meet the couple with the pug-nosed dog on the road.

"Hey, what's this about your bunny going missing?" the man says.

"It happened last night," I say. "Somehow he got out of the trailer."

"We can't find him anywhere," Libby says.

"I don't know if it helps, but we were out walking Brutus just after eight yesterday and noticed a couple kids—twins, I think—hanging around your trailer. Thought they were waiting for you two."

Sam and Libby and I exchange glances. Those twins!

"That does help!" I say. "More than you know!"

"Well, I hope you find him," the lady says.

"Thanks!" I say, and Sam and Libby and I take off running, heading for the twins' campsite.

At first it seems like no one's home. Then a loud snore comes from the tent trailer.

"Looks like we'll have to come back when everyone's up," I say, turning to go.

From behind, I hear the sound of a chain. I glance back just as Moose comes around the side of the tent. He takes one look at us and starts barking up a storm.

"Moose! Moose, shut up!" a sleepy voice yells from the tent trailer. "Jake? Logan? Shut him up."

The zipper on the small dome tent opens and one of the twins scrambles out and grabs Moose's chain. "Moose! Quiet!"

The dog stops barking, but doesn't take his eyes off us. Then the twin spots us and his eyes narrow. "What do you want?"

I cross my arms. "To talk."

"Who is it, Logan?" The other twin—Jake—crawls out of the tent. "Oh. You."

"We have nothing to say to you," Logan says.

"Oh, I think you do. And I think you need to come clean. Where's Tiny? Is he here?"

"If you hurt him—" Libby says, unable to finish her sentence because she's gulping back tears.

Sam puts her arm around her.

"I don't know what you're talking about." Logan sets his hands on his hips.

"Some neighbours saw you at our campsite last night," I say. "Don't try to pretend you don't know what I'm talking about. What did you do with Tiny?"

"We didn't do anything with your stupid rabbit," Jake says.

"Just tell us the truth," Sam says. "Where is he?"

"How should we know?" Jake says. "Maybe he opened the door and ran out into the woods on his own."

Logan shoots Jake a dirty look.

"He ran into the woods?" I say. "Which way?"

Jake crosses his arms. "I don't know what you're talking about."

"Would you just quit being such jerks and help us? How would you feel if it was Moose?"

"Your rabbit bit our dog. He's dangerous. Why should we help you?"

I throw my hands up in the air. "I give up."

Sam doesn't. "You tell us where Tiny is or maybe I should go knock on the trailer door and tell your dad what happened. How you went into a stranger's trailer, took their pet rabbit, and let it go in the woods." She nods her head toward the trailer and the loud snoring coming from inside.

"That's not how it happened!" Jake says.

"Shut up, Jake." Logan gives his brother an elbow.

"Look, we didn't mean to let him out," Jake continues. "We knocked on the door and thought someone answered, so we opened the door. He ran out before we could stop him. Then we couldn't catch him. We didn't know what to do, so we just left. We thought you'd find him when you got home."

"Jake!" Logan hisses.

"He went into the woods. That's the last time we saw him."

Sam, Libby, and I run back to our campsite as fast as we can.

"All right, we know he went into the woods. So let's start there."

We fan out and start searching the woods for clues. There's got to be something we missed. Then I spot it. Hanging from a bush is a clump of caramel-coloured fur.

"Sam! Libby!" I shout.

They come running.

"Look!"

"A clue!" Libby cries.

"He must've gone this way," I say, pointing deeper into the woods.

"All right," Sam says. "Libby you go to the left. I'll go to the right. Drew, you go to the centre. Don't go too fast and don't overlook anything, no matter how small you think it is."

We work our way through the woods, checking everything and anything that looks like a rabbit may have come this way.

"I found something!" Libby calls.

Sam and I hurry over to her. She's standing near a boggy spot by a fallen log. She points to what are very clearly rabbit tracks in the muddy ground.

"This way!" I say.

We find a few more clues and follow them. More hair caught on brambles. A few more tracks in the mud. They lead us to the edge of the woods. There's an old barbed wire fence and more of Tiny's fur is stuck to one of the rusty barbs. We help each other climb over, then push our way through a hedge of brambles and into a small field. There's a house and a small barn on the far side of it.

"Now where?" I say.

"I guess we go ask at that house," Sam says.

So obvious.

We push our way through the long grass until we find a path and follow it to the fence. No sooner do we reach it than a huge fluffy white dog comes around the front of the house and starts barking at us. *WOOF! WOOF! WOOF! WOOF!*

"Uh oh. Now what do we do?" I don't want to go into the yard with a dog like that. It would eat us for lunch and then look for a snack.

A lady comes out on the front porch, looking up the drive with her hand shielding her face. "Penny, what is it?"

The dog takes a few steps towards us, still woofing under its breath.

The lady turns to see what the dog is looking at and spots us. "Oh!"

"Um, hi," I say. "We're, um, looking for a rabbit?"

"A rabbit?" She says. "Well, you've come to the right place."

"Have you seen him?" Libby says, brightening. "Our bunny?"

"He's a Flemish Giant. Caramel-coloured. Big ears," I add.

"Why, as a matter of fact, yes. A rabbit of that description showed up last night. Penny found him. Come with me."

18
Hasenpfeffer

We follow the lady and the dog around the side of the house, past a chicken coop and a small field where some goats and a llama are grazing, and over to the small barn. There's a long row of rabbit hutches against the outside wall. The first hutch is larger than the others and has a bunch of baby rabbits in it—about the same size Tiny was when we got him. They're a mix of black, grey, and white, with caramel smudges. Some have faces that are half black and half white or grey. One has a perfect white stripe around the middle of its body. They crowd to the front of the cage as we walk past.

"Oh, they're so cute," Sam says, poking her finger through the wire mesh and scratching a little black-and-white-faced bunny on the nose. "How old are they?"

"Coming up on three and a half months."

"What's their breed?"

"Just a mix. Their father was a New Zealand cross. Their mother here, Hasenpfeffer, is part Flemish, part French Lop."

"Hasenpfeffer?" I say, trying to wrap my mouth around the word. "That's a funny name."

"It's German for rabbit stew," the lady says, with a wink.

"That's not—!" Libby starts to say, so I step on her foot.

The lady was nice enough to find Tiny. We don't need to criticize her choice in rabbit names.

"Ouch! Drew!" she says. "What did you do that for?"

"Whoops! Sorry, didn't see you there."

She gives me a look that says she wishes she didn't have an older brother and was an only child instead. But at least she doesn't say anything.

I glance at Hasenpfeffer, lying curled up in the corner in the next hutch. She's the same colour as the babies, except she's got a wide white stripe down her face and a white dewlap—the roll of fat under her chin most female rabbits have. She's a big rabbit, like Tiny. Only she's got one ear that lops down, while the other stands up. She turns the upright ear in my direction, but doesn't move. Poor Hasenpfeffer. Not much of a life stuck outside in a tiny hutch.

In the last hutch, we find Tiny. He's got his nose and front feet pressed against the door, looking both overjoyed to see us and quite displeased with being penned up again.

"Tiny!" Libby cries and bursts into tears.

The lady opens the hutch and the rabbit practically jumps into Libby's arms, nearly knocking her off her feet.

"Oh, Tiny you scared us so much!" Libby sobs into his fur.

I scratch his forehead and he tooth-purrs. "I think he's happy we found him," I say.

"I would say so, too," the lady says. "He seems quite attached to you."

I take the rabbit from Libby and give him a hug. He plants his front feet on my shoulders like he always does and nibbles the top of my hair. "Stop it, you silly rabbit," I say.

"Well, this is a happy result," the lady says. "We had no idea where he came from. Just appeared in the yard yesterday after dinner. Penny found him. If no one claimed him, we were thinking of keeping him. He'd make pretty babies."

"Tiny can't have babies," Libby says. "He's fixed."

"Fixed?" the lady says. "As in neutered?"

"Yeah," I say. "Just like a dog or cat." I think about the day Mom took Tiny to the vet and brought him

home all wobbly and sore. Fortunately, he forgave us pretty quick, but he no longer likes the vet very much.

The lady shakes her head in disbelief. "I didn't know you could neuter rabbits."

"Me either," says Sam.

Libby takes the opportunity to explain the benefits of spaying and neutering pet rabbits. I'm pretty sure she's got *The Ultimate House Rabbit Guide Book* memorized by now because what she's saying sounds like it came straight from the pages.

"Thanks so much for catching him for us," I say to the lady. "We were so worried about him last night, thinking he was out in the woods all by himself."

"Thank Penny. She found him. Didn't you, Penny?"

Penny wags her big fluffy tail.

"Do you want to give her a cookie?" the lady asks us.

Libby grins. "If she found Tiny, then she *deserves* a cookie."

Penny's tail wags some more at the word "cookie."

We walk back to the porch and the lady pulls out a big tin from just inside the back door. She takes off the lid and holds it out to us. We each take a bone-shaped dog cookie.

"Okay," the lady instructs us. "Tell Penny to sit."

"Sit!" Libby says and giggles when Penny sits. She holds out the cookie and the dog takes it gingerly from her fingers and then *CHOMP! CHOMP! CRUNCH!* she swallows it without dropping a single crumb. She looks at Libby for more.

"She seems to like you," the lady says. "Not all Great Pyrenees warm up to strangers so quickly."

Sam and I feed her our cookies. She gobbles them up like they're the first dog cookies she's ever tasted.

"Okay, that's probably enough for now." The lady pets Penny's large head. "Such a good girl, Penny."

We thank the lady again for finding Tiny and head back to the campground. The lady tells us if we go up to the road and turn right it'll lead us back to the front gate and we don't have to go tromping through the woods again. We follow her instructions, and sure enough we find ourselves just outside the entrance to the campground.

"Those baby bunnies are so adorable," Sam says. "I wonder if they're for sale. I bet Daddy would let me get one."

"They're not for sale," Libby says.

"How do you know?" I say.

"Because she's going to eat them. They're meat rabbits, Drew. Don't you know anything?"

"You don't know that."

"Well, they're not show rabbits and they're not wool rabbits, so what else would they be for?"

She has a point. "Maybe she just likes having them around?" I say.

Libby just rolls her eyes at me.

"I'm going to ask Daddy if I can get one," Sam says. "I bet she wouldn't say no if we offered her enough money."

I smile at the idea of Sam getting a rabbit.

"I like the little one with the white stripe around his middle," she continues. "I'd call him Oreo."

She and Libby talk about rabbits as we walk back to the campsite. As we pass the camp store, the campground worker spots us. "Hey, you found your bunny!"

"We sure did!"

"Where was he?"

"At the farm with the rabbits."

"Well, there you go!" he laughs and pats Tiny on the head and then walks off to stack more wood in the wheelbarrows in front of the store.

The boys with bikes spot us next. They crowd around to pet the rabbit.

"Tiny!"

"You found him!"

"Yay!"

We are quite the parade through the campground as more and more kids spot us and come out to congratulate us and pet Tiny.

Then I spot two kids I know aren't going to be happy for us. The twins are skulking down the road, shooting us dirty looks.

Libby and Sam spot them, too.

"Come on," I say.

We march right past them, without saying a word. They watch us go and for the first time since we met them they have nothing to say.

"Hey, what time is it?" I ask Sam when we're around the next corner.

She pulls out her iPhone. "Ten forty-five."

"Yikes! We better get going. Nana and Papa will be wondering where we are! We're moving to a new campsite by the beach."

"Sweet!" she says. "Catch you later?"

"Sure thing!"

Libby and I run back to the campsite as fast as we can.

The trailer is already hooked up to the truck when we get there. Nana's sitting in the front seat. Papa is just checking the bungee cords holding my bike to the back.

"Oh, you found him!" Nana cries, climbing out of the truck as soon as she spots us.

"Yup!" I grin. "He was at a farm on the other side of the woods."

"A farm?" Nana says.

"Just over there." I point.

"You don't say?" Papa says.

"A lady found him and put him in a cage with some other rabbits."

"They're going to eat them!" Libby says. "We have to save them."

"What do you mean, 'save them'?" Papa says.

"We can buy them off the lady," Libby says. "Sam says they'll sell them if we have enough money. Drew has money from his paper route we can use."

I do?

"Libby," Nana says. "You'd have to get permission from your mom and dad before you got another rabbit."

"Isn't one enough?" Papa says.

"But they'll eat them!" Libby wails. "They're just babies."

"How many rabbits are we talking about?" Papa says.

"I didn't count," I say, "but I think there's at least a dozen babies and one mother."

"I counted. There are nine babies," Libby says.

"Ten rabbits? You want to buy ten rabbits and bring them home? Oh, Libby," Nana says.

Then Nana and Papa proceed to give Libby a talk about life and how things aren't always fair and how farms work and that as long as the rabbits aren't suffering, they're not going to do anything about it.

Libby's lower lip sticks out further and further and further.

"Well, at least Tiny is home safe and sound." Papa says. "All's well that ends well."

"Better get him back in his cage," Nana says. She opens the trailer door.

With the slide in place, there's not much space to walk inside. Tiny's cage is squished between the side of the couch and the bedroom door.

"In you go, Tiny," I say, putting him into his cage and latching it. He rattles the bars a bit, then spots his food bowl and decides he'd rather eat.

We close the trailer door and climb into the truck.

"Beachfront property, here we come!" Papa says, and we pull out of the campsite and onto the road. Goodbye, mosquitos. Goodbye, squirrels. Goodbye, stinky outhouses. Hello, beach!

19
Fore!

Just as the campground worker promised, the campsite next to Ralph and Sheila's RV is empty. Papa backs the trailer into place and unhooks the truck. We climb out and help him get everything set up again: extending the slide and the awning, moving the picnic table up against the trailer, setting up the lawn chairs around the fire pit facing the beach, and getting my bike down.

"Can we go to the beach now? Please, please, *please*?" I say, not caring that I sound like Libby. The weather is perfect. Only a few puffy clouds in the sky. The sun is warm and the deep blue-grey water looks inviting. There are a ton of people already down on the beach, building sandcastles, jumping waves, throwing Frisbees, flying kites, tossing sticks for their dogs to chase.

"We will," Papa says. "But first, I think it's time you learned to play golf."

Golf? Uh oh! My mind flashes back to the first day we were here and Papa's broken golf club. We can't play golf. He'll find out I broke his club.

"I'm, uh, feeling a bit tired," I say with an exaggerated yawn. "I didn't sleep so good last night. I was thinking of taking a nap."

Papa raises his bushy eyebrows. "I thought you wanted to go to the beach?"

"Yeah, uh, that's what I meant. Taking a nap. On the beach."

"There's plenty of time for that later," Papa says. "The beach isn't going anywhere, but our one o'clock tee time won't wait."

"It'll be good for you and Papa to spend some time together," Nana says, giving me an encouraging smile.

"What about the toilet?"

"What about it?"

"Well, isn't the part supposed to be here today? Shouldn't we go to town and get it? Then we can spend the afternoon fixing it together."

"I already called this morning, Drew. It's not here yet. They'll let us know when it comes in."

I plop down at the table. "We'll be going home before that happens," I grumble.

"That's a strong possibility," Papa agrees, shaking

his head. "But there's not much we can do about it, now, can we?"

"You'll have fun, Drew," Nana says, ruffling my hair.

"Can't Libby go? I bet she wants to learn how to play golf."

Libby gives me a look like I've just started speaking alien. "No, I want to stay here with Nana."

"Libby and I are going to have some girl time," Nana says.

"But—"

"No buts!" Nana says, opening the fridge and pulling out some sliced meat and bread. "I'll make us some lunch and then you can go."

Ugh.

🥕 🥕 🥕

After we eat, Papa goes into the bedroom to change. He comes out wearing orange and brown plaid pants, a pink shirt, and a white straw hat with a black band. In his hand is a pair of white and green golf shoes with metal studs on the soles.

"That's what you're going to wear?" I say.

"You betcha. Got my lucky shirt, my lucky pants, and my lucky hat. And, of course, my lucky golf club in my bag."

"How much luck do you need to play golf?"

"All the luck in the world." He winks at me. "Now let's get going."

We load up Papa's golf clubs into the truck, climb in, and head for the golf course. The whole way there, Papa talks about golf. The rules. The technique. How much fun it is. I try to pay attention, but after the first little bit it all sounds like *blah, blah, blah.* All I can think about is the broken golf club in the bag in the back of the truck. It's only a matter of time before Papa finds it. I don't want to get in trouble, but I also know what happens when you don't tell the truth.

We pull into the parking lot and climb out. Papa leads the way into the clubhouse where we pay our fee, then head out to the start of the course. If I'd ever wondered what it felt like to be a prisoner on death row taking his last walk to the execution chamber, this was it.

"This is the tee," Papa says, handing me a golf ball and a little white peg. "You'll want to start here between the green tees, since you're a beginner." He shows me how to poke the peg, also called a "tee," into the ground and set the ball on top of it. "Now we'll choose a club."

My heart starts to beat faster. I just know he's going to grab the club I broke.

"There are many different types of clubs. You've got your woods, your irons, your chippers, and, of course, your putter." He pulls each club out and tells me which it is and what it's used for. My heart beats faster and faster, just waiting for him to pull out the club I've broken. Sweat beads on my forehead. At last he comes to the broken club. "And, most importantly, you've got to have a lucky club."

I think I might faint. His lucky club. Of all the golf clubs in his bag, I had to break his lucky club.

"You okay, Drew? You look a little pale."

"I, uh," I stammer. Then I take a deep breath. "Papa, there's something I need to tell you."

"You aren't going to throw up again, are you?"

"No, nothing like that."

"This isn't another excuse, is it?"

"No."

"Well, can it wait?" Papa glances over to a group of other golfers lining up their bags for their turn at the tee. "We're holding up the show."

I swallow. "Uh, I guess."

He hands me a golf club with a big wooden head. "All right, here's how you hold it." He shows me how to lace my fingers around the grip. Then he stands behind me and shows me how to swing the club to hit the ball. *CHOCK!* It flies through the air and lands in the grass in the middle of the fairway.

"Well, done, Drew!" Papa says.

I give him a weak grin. It's hard to be excited about my golfing abilities when I know how this game is going to end. Probably with yelling. Possibly grounding.

And most definitely me paying to replace Papa's golf club. As if you can replace a lucky club. Ugh.

"Now it's my turn. Stand back." He tees up his ball and then *THWACK!* sends his ball flying about three times as far as mine. "Fore!" he yells.

Then he nods to the group of other golfers and grabs his clubs. "Okay, let's go."

We head off down the fairway, Papa chatting about golf, me feeling like my stomach is sinking into my knees.

When we get to my ball, he goes for the clubs again. "Now you need an iron." He pulls out a metal club and hands it to me. "All right, give it a good whack."

I can't stand it. "Papa, can I please tell you something?"

"Concentrate, Drew."

Ugh.

I try to tell Papa a few more times as we continue the game, but each time he's got a reason not to hear me out:

"No talking on the back swing."

"Are you paying attention? Putting is important."

"Just keep looking. We'll find your ball."

Ugh.

Finally, I can't take it anymore. We're halfway through the course and I'm so sick with dread, I feel like I could barf again. And I really don't want to barf again.

"Papa," I say. "I broke your lucky golf club."

Papa looks at me with a strange look on his face. "You what?"

"I broke your golf club. I know I shouldn't have touched it, but it was the first thing I saw, so I grabbed it. I had to protect Libby and Tiny from that horrible dog, Moose. I'm really sorry. I know it won't be your lucky club, but I promise I'll pay for a new one."

Papa just keeps looking at me. "How could you break it?"

"I didn't mean to. I hit the picnic table. I was trying to scare them off."

"Drew, you couldn't have broken it. It's already broken!"

I blink. "Um, what?"

He pulls the club from the bag and pops the handle from the metal shaft. "See. Already broken."

My jaw drops. "But ... how ... what?"

Papa laughs his big booming laugh. "I call it my lucky golf club because I broke it myself many years ago. Got a double eagle for the first time in my life—the only time, truth be told—so I kept the club for good luck."

I don't know what to say. I just stand there gaping at him.

"I'm glad you told me the truth, Drew. But really, it's nothing to worry about." Papa squeezes my shoulder. "Come on, let's play some golf."

We finish the game and I actually have some fun. Golf isn't easy, but it's challenging in a good way. And Papa is a good teacher. He makes it fun and even when I get my ball stuck in a sand trap and it takes a thousand swings to get it out, he doesn't get impatient. "Practice makes perfect," he says.

When the game is over, rather than head straight back to the campground, Papa says, "Y'know, maybe we should check and see if that part for the toilet has arrived. I'm about tired of having to trek out in the middle of the night to use the outhouse."

I could not agree with him more.

We drive to the hardware store. The man at the counter greets us. "You're in luck. It just arrived." He goes to the back room and brings back a box and hands it to Papa.

"Good thing I wore my lucky golf clothes." Papa winks at me, then adjusts his glasses to read the box. "Oh, hang on. This is the wrong part."

"It is?" The man takes the box back and compares it with the order form. "You're right, it is. I'm terribly sorry." He starts tapping keys on the computer. "I'll have to reorder the correct part. It'll be here tomorrow."

Ugh. We're never going to have a working toilet again.

20
Poor Little Princess

The trailer smells somewhere between a hair salon and a paint store when we get back.

"Look, Drew!" Libby holds out her hands. "Nana did my nails!"

Her fingernails are a bright pink with little rabbit faces painted in black and white onto them.

"Great, Libby."

"It's called a mandacure."

"I think you mean 'manicure.'"

"She did my toes, too. And look! I'm wearing make-up." She bats her eyelashes at me. She's got blue make-up on her eyes, red on her cheeks, and her lips are a shiny pink gloss. She looks ridiculous.

"Good for you."

"We had so much fun, didn't we, Nana?"

Nana beams at Libby. "We did."

"Did you have fun golfing?" Libby asks.

"Yup," I say.

"Did you get in trouble?" She drops her voice to a whisper. "About the golf club. You know, the one you broke?"

"You can't break something that's already broken," I say.

Libby looks confused.

"I broke it," Papa says. "A long time ago."

"So, Drew's not in trouble?"

"Not unless he's done something else I don't know about." He gives me a fake stern look.

"How's Tiny?" I ask, changing the subject. "He looks kind of sad."

Even though the door is wide open, Tiny is hunched in the corner of his cage, his ears down.

"He misses the other bunnies," Libby says.

"How can you be so sure? Maybe he's just tired of camping and wants to go home."

Libby doesn't look convinced. "He's lonely. He wants a friend."

Just then, a car comes roaring up the road outside. It's Ralph and Sheila's. It comes to a stop between our campsite and theirs and then Ralph jumps out of the driver's seat and runs around and helps Sheila from the car. She doesn't look too good.

"Oh dear," Nana says and rushes outside to see if she can help.

We follow after her.

"Everything all right?" Nana says.

"We're fine." Sheila pushes Nana away. "Mind your own business."

Nana steps back like she's just received an electric shock.

"Just a little sea sickness," Ralph says as Sheila leans over and barfs into the nearest bush.

"Looks more like stomach flu to me." Nana crosses her arms.

"It was a bit choppy out there. She'll be better if she can just lie down." Ralph helps Sheila into their RV and shuts the door.

Their little dog is still sitting in the front seat of the car, shaking like a leaf.

"Hey! You forgot your dog," I say.

Nana picks her up and shuts the car door.

"Poor little Princess," Libby says and pats the dog on the head.

Princess licks Libby's hand, making her giggle.

A minute later, Ralph comes back out to get the dog.

"Thanks," he says, though he doesn't look grateful in the least. Just annoyed. Then he goes back into the RV, slamming the door behind him.

We're just about to head back into the trailer, when

Gord and Brenda arrive. They park their truck at their campsite and come over.

"What a nightmare." Gord shakes his head. "First we end up late because we're waiting for you guys to show up. Then the pet stroller breaks on the trail halfway to the hot springs, so Ralph and I end up packing it there and back. Then Sheila gets sick on the boat ride home. And to top it all off, no whales. Not a single one."

And here I was complaining about having to play golf. That trip sounds plain awful.

"Did you find the bunny?" Brenda asks.

"We did, thankfully." Nana nods. "He turned up at a farm just up the road from here. The kids tracked him down."

"Oh, well, that's good to hear. You'll need to keep a closer eye on him," she says to me and Libby.

"We will, for sure," I say. "No more escaping rabbits."

Gord and Brenda head off to get some dinner. "Stop by later if you like," Gord says.

"What about the Friday Night Market?" Papa says.

"Cancelled."

"Well, I've got to be honest, that's a relief," Nana says as we head back to the trailer. "So, who wants hamburgers?"

I know I do!

We're just sitting down at the picnic table with our

dinner when Ralph comes out of the RV. He pops the trunk on their car and pulls out the folded-up pink pet stroller. He slams the trunk and heads up the road with it.

"Mr. Ralph!" Libby cries, jumping up from the table to chase after him.

"Libby!" Nana says. "Sit down."

"Mr. Ralph! What are you going to do with the pet stroller?"

Ralph stops and turns toward Libby. "I'm throwing it in the trash. It's broken." He gives it a shake and the wheel—the one that popped off while I was using it for garbage duty—wobbles like it's about to fall off again.

"Well, can I have it then?" Libby asks, giving Ralph her cookies and ice cream look.

"Suit yourself," he says. "You know where the dumpster is as well as I do." Then he shoves the pet stroller at Libby and stomps back to the RV.

Papa gets up to help her. "What on earth are you going to do with this?"

"Tiny can ride in it! Then we don't have to worry about dogs chasing him or him running off and getting lost."

"But it's broken."

"We can fix it, can't we, Papa?" she says.

Papa takes a closer look at the wobbly wheel. "Y'know," he says. "I think this just needs a C clip and it'll be right as rain again. Let me check my tool box."

He carries the stroller back to our campsite and sets it by the picnic table. Then he pulls out his toolbox from the cubby in the trailer, rummages around inside it for a minute, and pulls out a small metal clip. He flips the stroller onto its side, pops off the little plastic cap holding the wheel in place, then slides the clip into its place. He spins the wheel. No more wobbles.

Libby jumps up and down and claps her hands. "Papa, you fixed it! You fixed it!" She wraps her arms around him. "You're the best Papa in the world."

"Well ..." Papa says.

Libby lets him go. "We have to get Tiny!"

"Hold on now." Nana catches her arm. "I think it's time you sat down and had something to eat first. Tiny can wait."

Libby plunks down at the picnic table. "But I'm not hungry."

"Well, I know I am," I say, taking a giant bite of my hamburger. "If I finish first, does that mean I get to push the pet stroller?"

"No-o!" Libby grabs her hamburger and starts eating as fast as she can. "I get to push it first!"

Nana gives me a smile that says "thank you."

I smile back at her. Like I'd be caught dead pushing a rabbit in a pink pet stroller.

After dinner, Libby and I help Nana wash up the dishes, then we get Tiny from his cage and put him into the pet stroller and zip it closed. He has no idea what to think of it. As soon as it starts moving, his eyes get really big and he spreads his feet out like the floor is about to drop out from under him.

"Let's take him to the park," Libby says.

"The park? How about we just walk him around here?"

"Nana! Drew won't go to the park with me!"

Nana pops her head out the trailer door. "Take your sister to the park, Drew."

Ugh.

"Can I at least take my bike?"

"Don't forget your helmet."

Ralph comes out of the RV to move the car into its proper parking spot. "I see you fixed the stroller."

"Papa did!" Libby beams.

"You don't want it back now, do you?" I ask.

"That piece of junk? No thank you. It's only a matter of time before the other wheels pop off."

He gets in the car and slams the door.

I feel a bit guilty. The wheel probably wouldn't have popped off if I hadn't used it to move those big heavy bags of garbage. Of course, I wouldn't have had to use it if the bags of garbage hadn't weighed a ton to begin with.

"Come on, Drew. Tiny wants to go eat grass."

I pedal after Libby to the park.

We spend the rest of the day there. I ride my bike with the other boys and even a few girls that join us. Libby sits on the grass with Tiny and talks to anyone who'll stay long enough to listen about rabbits. At one point she's got half a dozen kids and even a couple moms listening to her. If we were smart, we'd start charging money to hear her talk. We could call it *Libby's Lagomorph Lessons.*

When it starts to get dark, Nana finds us and calls us home. For the second time on our trip, I actually go to bed happy.

21
Cookies

"Drew!"

I wake with a start. "Wha—? Huh?"

Libby's face is inches from mine. "Drew! I need to go pee!"

Ugh. "Hang on." I climb out of bed, get my hoodie, and find a couple flashlights from the drawer. "Didn't you go before bed?"

"Yeah, but I have to go again."

I glance out the kitchen window. The sky is changing from pitch black to a dark grey. The clock on the microwave reads 3:36. Ugh.

"Can't you go by yourself? It's almost morning."

"No, I'm too scared."

Ugh. "Come on."

I stuff my feet into my flip-flops and we head outside to the bathroom at the park. At least it's not as far of a walk as it used to be. Just on the other side of the long row of campsites opposite the beachfront sites.

As we pass Ralph and Sheila's RV, I notice the lights are on. Then the door opens and Sheila comes stomping out.

"I'm not an invalid, Ralph. I can walk. Just hurry up and get me to the emergency room."

She spots us and stops. "What are you doing here?"

"Just going to the bathroom," I say, pointing towards the park.

"Well, don't stand there gawking," she snaps. "Get going." She climbs into the car and slams the door. Through the back window I can see her applying lipstick in the visor mirror.

"You heard her," I say to Libby.

We head on down the road to the park. As we round the corner, Ralph and Sheila's car backs out and roars up the road in the opposite direction.

"All right, be quick," I say when we get to the bathrooms.

Libby heads into the ladies' room. I wait outside. It's dead quiet out, aside from the sound of the wind and the waves and Libby singing "Let It Go" in the bathroom. Ugh.

I wait a few minutes, then decide I have to go, too. I head into the men's room.

When I come out, there's no sign of Libby. "Libby?" I say in a loud whisper. "You done?"

No sound from the ladies' washroom. Ugh. Now what has she done? Fallen in the toilet and drowned?

I push open the door to the ladies' room. "Libby?" I check the stalls. No Libby. Where is that girl? I'm just heading for the door to go back outside, when it swings open. The same lady who caught me in the ladies' room the second day we were here is standing there in her pyjamas and a sweater.

"Again?" she says.

"Um, have you seen my sister?"

"Just get out of here!" She holds the door for me.

I slink out. Ugh. So embarrassing.

"If I catch you in here again, I'm telling the manager." She lets the door bang shut.

Trust me. I never plan to go into the ladies' room again.

"Libby?" I call. "Libby, where are you?" I pull out my flashlight and shine it around. No Libby. Did she suddenly turn into the Cowardly Lion at the end of *The Wizard of Oz* and get brave and walk home on her own? My mind is going a mile a minute. Libby wouldn't go off with anyone, would she? She'd scream for sure if someone tried to kidnap her, right? I glance around, trying to find some hint as to where she's gone. Then I spot it. A flash of light in the trees. It's a flashlight beam, bouncing along the trail leading away from the park, back toward our old campsite.

Libby! I hurry after her and catch up just as she reaches the road.

"What are you doing? I thought you were too scared to go out alone at night?"

"I'm going to save the bunnies."

"In the dark."

"Duh."

"Libby, you can't just go onto someone's property and steal their rabbits."

"It's not stealing. I'm going to rescue them. She's going to *eat* them, Drew."

"You don't know that!"

"And you don't know she won't!" Libby crosses her arms.

"Look, Libby, I'd love to save the baby bunnies as much as you, but we can't go stealing other people's rabbits. It's wrong. And then what would we do with them when we got them home? Put them in your bed?"

"No-o!" She crosses her arms.

I can totally tell that was her plan. I shake my head. "It's just not going to work. Now come on, we need to get back to the campsite. Nana and Papa might wake up and wonder where we are." I start walking back down the gravel path towards the park.

"Andrew Wayne Montgomery," Libby says in her best Nana voice. "If you don't help me rescue those bunnies I'm going to tell all your friends at home you have a girlfriend."

I spin around. "Sam is *not* my girlfriend."

"Oh, really? Then why were you kissing behind the outhouses?"

"We weren't kissing! We were *talking*!"

"It sounded like kissing to me. I bet Quentin wants me to tell him all about it."

Ugh. For a while, all the guys in grade six thought Tabitha was my girlfriend and not *just* my friend and wouldn't stop making fun of me. Like I want to go through that again.

"Fine. You win. We'll rescue the rabbits. But we need a *real* plan."

🥕   🥕   🥕

"This better work or we are both dead meat," I say.

Libby and I are standing at the end of the lady's driveway. We can already hear Penny barking back at the house. *WOOF! WOOF! WOOF! WOOF!*

"It'll work, Drew. I'm positive," Libby says and starts pushing the pet stroller down the rutted driveway.

Penny's barking is getting closer. We round a bend and can see the dark silhouette of the house at the end of the driveway. Penny's large white shape is moving toward us, still barking.

"Penny! Hi, Penny!" Libby says. "Guess what we've got for you! Do you want a cookie?"

Penny stops about five feet away from us, still barking. *WOOF! WOOF! WOOF!* She seems confused.

"Sit, Penny!" Libby pulls a dog cookie from her pocket. I don't know how she did it, but somehow she managed to scoop extra dog cookies from the tin this morning and stuck them in her pocket without anyone noticing. "Sit, Penny. Come on. Good girl."

Penny's barking slows. *WOOF!* She licks her lips. A line of drool is forming at the corner of her mouth. *WOOF!*

"Remember us?" I say. "We gave you cookies. You like cookies, right?"

Finally Penny stops barking and comes forward to sniff the cookie in Libby's hand.

"Sit," Libby says.

Penny sits.

"Okay, here you go," Libby says and gives the dog the cookie.

CHOMP! CHOMP! CRUNCH! Penny gobbles it up and sniffs Libby's hand for more.

Libby giggles. "You better give her one, too," Libby says, giving me a cookie.

I hold it out to Penny. She gobbles it up just as fast as the first one.

"Good girl," Libby says, petting the dog on her large head.

Penny waves her fluffy tail and gazes up at Libby with adoring eyes.

"All right." I take a deep breath. "Let's get this done before we get caught."

We head for the barn with Penny leading the way. She keeps glancing back at us like she can't quite figure out what we're doing. I'm not entirely sure we know what we're doing, either.

At the barn, Libby goes straight to the hutch with the baby rabbits and opens it. The babies come hopping forward, looking for treats.

"Guess we should've brought some carrots or banana," I say.

Libby pulls a handful of rabbit pellets from her pocket. Of course. My sister the brainiac.

She holds out her hand to the bunnies and they start gobbling up the pellets.

"Their whiskers tickle," she giggles.

I glance around nervously. "Okay, enough fooling around. Let's get these bunnies and go." I unzip the stroller, scoop up one of the bunnies and plop it inside.

A low growl comes from Penny.

Uh oh.

"Uh, Libby?"

But again, she's a step ahead of me. "It's okay, Penny. You want another cookie?"

Penny wags her tail.

While Libby feeds Penny every last cookie in her pocket, I grab bunnies and stick them in the stroller. Last, I get Hasenpfeffer. She doesn't seem too impressed about being picked up, but she's happy to be reunited with her babies. She sniffs them over like she's checking to make sure I didn't hurt them.

"Okay, got 'em. Let's go!"

"Wait!"

"What? Why?"

Libby pulls the notepad from the kitchen out of her pocket and a pen and writes:

Its rong to eat bunies. We will geve them a gode hom and will take gode car of them.

She sticks the note in Hasenpfeffer's hutch. Then we hurry back to the road as fast as the stroller can go without the wheel popping off again.

"Bye, Penny!" Libby says when we get to the road. "You be a good girl, okay?" She feeds her one last cookie, pats her on the head, then we race back to the campground.

The sky is just turning pink and yellow to the east when we get back to our campsite.

"I really hope Nana and Papa are still asleep," I say, eyeing the darkened trailer nervously. "If they wake up now, we are so dead."

Just then, a light flicks on inside.

"Quick! Hide!"

We duck behind the truck.

"Now what do we do?" I say, peeking over the hood at the trailer. I can see Papa shuffling into the kitchen. It's only a matter of time before he notices we're not in bed and comes looking for us.

"We'll put them in Ralph and Sheila's RV," Libby says.

"We'll *what*?" I gape at her. "Have you gone crazy? They'll kill us!"

"It'll only be for a little while. Just until we tell Nana and Papa."

"Yeah, about that. You're on your own there. This was your idea. Not mine. I only agreed to help because you didn't give me any other choice."

We sneak over to the RV with the pet stroller and try the door.

"It's locked." I shrug. "So much for that plan."

"Help me find the key, Drew." Libby starts poking around under the RV.

"Key? What key?"

"Got it!" She pulls a small magnetized box from underneath, pops it open, and pulls out a key.

"How did you—?"

She rolls her eyes at me like I'm an idiot. "It's a hide-a-key. I saw it on TV."

"But how did you know Ralph and Sheila would have one?"

She shrugs. "Why wouldn't they?"

Good point. Sheila's got everything. Of course she would have an extra key.

We unlock the RV and sneak inside. It's dark and I can't see anything. I trip on something and it yelps. Princess. They've left poor Princess here in the dark.

"Sorry, Princess," I say. "You okay?"

I don't want to turn on a light, so I shine my flashlight around in search of the dog. Whoa. This place is fancy. Leather couch, glass top table and chairs, gleaming white kitchen, even a fireplace. The dog is hiding under the dining table, quivering with fear. "Hey, we brought you some friends," I say.

Libby is already bringing rabbits inside. She hands me a bunny.

"Where do we put them?" I say.

"Let's put them in the bathroom."

I find the bathroom at the back of the RV. It's as fancy as the rest of the place. Big glass shower, huge mirror, polished chrome, even a washer and dryer.

I set the rabbit down, then take another from Libby.

"You think they'll be okay on the floor? There's no tub."

"We'll put some towels down so they don't slip." Libby grabs some fluffy white towels from a rack and lays them on the floor. One of the babies hops right onto it and starts digging at it.

"Hey! No!" I shoo it away. "You sure that's a good idea? If these are Sheila's good towels, we're dead." I open the cupboard under the sink, but can't find any towels that are any less white or fluffy.

"We can wash them later, Drew." Libby points at the washing machine. "We don't even have to go to the laundry."

She has a point. "Okay, let's just get the rest of the rabbits and get out of here."

Fast as we can, we unload all the bunnies. Hasenpfeffer is last. She thumps loudly when we set her down. Her not-lop ear is standing straight up and her lop ear is pointing forward. She looks funny, like a helicopter. She begins sniffing around the bathroom, checking out her new temporary home. She bumps noses with one of her babies, then starts washing its ears.

"Oh, look how cute they are, Drew!" Libby squeals.

I have to admit, they are pretty cute. But we can't stick around all day watching them. "What about food? Or a litter box?" I say.

Libby pulls another handful of rabbit pellets from her pocket and sprinkles it onto the towels covering the floor. The bunnies go crazy trying to gobble it up.

"That's all I've got." She shrugs.

"What? Nothing else in your magic pockets?" I say.

She glares at me. "Maybe there's some vegetables in the fridge?"

"Libby! It's bad enough we're hiding bunnies in Ralph and Sheila's bathroom. Now you want to take their vegetables, too?"

"Just a few. They won't even notice."

Ugh.

We check out the fridge. There's not much for vegetables, but we find some fancy salad in a bag that looks like it's starting to wilt. "Here, we can give them this," I say. "Sheila's probably just going to throw it out, anyway."

We feed the rabbits the salad, then hurry out of the RV, giving Princess a reassuring pat on the way. "We'll be back for them soon," I say. Hopefully long before Ralph and Sheila come back. The Tofino emergency room better be super busy tonight.

Then we lock the door, tuck the key back in its hiding spot, and hurry over to our campsite. The light is out in the kitchen. Libby parks the stroller by the door and we sneak inside. It's dead quiet, except for Papa snoring in the bedroom. Maybe he didn't notice us gone after all.

22
Criminals

I awaken to a screeching sound. At first, I think it's the tsunami sirens going off, then my brain comes all the way awake and I realize it's coming from just outside my window. I pull back the curtain. Sheila and Ralph are on their way over. Sheila looks hopping mad. Ralph is sneezing his head off. Oh no! The bunnies. They must've found the bunnies. I drag my pillow over my head. Maybe I'll suffocate to death before they can kill me.

"What on earth...?" Papa says.

He and Nana are drinking coffee at the table. He gets up just as our unhappy visitors bang loudly on the trailer door. Papa opens the door to a blast of Sheila's angry words.

"Where are those children?"

"They're still in bed. Why?"

"There are rabbits in my bathroom!"

"Rabbits?" Papa says with a mix of shock and disbelief.

"Yes! Rabbits! A big one and at least a dozen little ones! And they've messed all over the floor and ruined my towels!"

"There's hair everywhere!" Ralph adds, just as a sneezing fit overwhelms him.

"Drew?! Libby?!" Nana's voice is sharp. "You better get up and tell us what you know about this!"

"Talk to Libby," I say from under the pillow. "It was her idea."

"You helped!" Libby says, climbing out of her bunk.

Gee, thanks, Libby. "Only because you blackmailed me." I crawl out of bed, ready to meet my doom.

Nana's arms are crossed, her mouth a tight line. Papa has a dark scowl on his face. I can't even look at Ralph or Sheila. I'm too scared.

"Well?" Nana says.

I give Libby a prod. "You tell them. It was your idea."

Libby gives me a hateful look. "We had to rescue the bunnies," she says. "That lady was going to eat them."

"Libby, we talked about this—" Nana starts to say but Sheila cuts her off.

"Then you should have let her!" Her eyes flash with anger. "What right did you have to put *rabbits* in *my* bathroom?!"

"It was just supposed to be for a little while," Libby says quietly. "Until we could talk to Nana and Papa about it."

"We had to put them somewhere," I say. "The bathroom seemed the best place."

"Those were Egyptian cotton bath towels!" Sheila screeches. "I should call the police! Charge you both with breaking and entering! Property damage!" She waves the empty salad bag. "Theft!"

Libby starts to cry.

Nana puts her arm around her. "Now Sheila, let's not be so drastic."

"We didn't break in," I say. "We found your hide-a-key."

"What?! How?" Ralph says.

"It wasn't hidden very good," Libby says, sniffling.

"It doesn't matter!" Sheila snaps at us. "You didn't have permission! You had no business going into our property! I should call 9-1-1 right now!"

"You are not going to call the police," Papa says. "They're children. They made a mistake."

"A mistake?! You bet they made a mistake! They made the biggest mistake of their life!" Sheila is getting louder and louder. I swear the whole campground can hear her.

"Sheila, please. You need to calm down," Papa says.

"No!" She stabs a finger at Papa. "You need to keep

these children in line. They've done nothing but cause trouble this entire trip. I've tried to be accommodating. Tried to include them in the activities. Tried to be reasonable. And this is how they repay me? Enough! I want those rabbits out of my RV and I want them out now!" Then she turns and stomps away, Ralph following after her, still sneezing.

"You heard her," Nana says. "Go get the rabbits."

"Come with us, Nana? Please?" Libby says. "She's scary."

"Don't worry," Papa says. "We wouldn't leave you alone with her for a second."

We troop out of the trailer and over to the RV. Libby brings the pet stroller, and we round up the bunnies and put them back into it. The bathroom is a real mess. Pee and poop everywhere. We really should've made an effort to find a litter box for them. The towels are ruined. They've got little holes nibbled all over them.

"I expect you to pay to replace those," Sheila says. "They're Ralph Lauren."

Nana makes a sound like a strangled gurgle. "No," she says. "They will not pay to replace your towels. Who in their right mind brings Ralph Lauren towels camping?"

Sheila huffs and puffs. "Just get out. Take your little vermin and get out."

"Wait!" Libby cries. "There's one missing!"

"What?" I say.

"A baby is missing!" Libby says. "There should be nine, but there's only eight!"

We search the RV.

"Found it!" Papa cries, from Ralph and Sheila's bedroom.

We run to the room just in time to see a little black and grey mottled bunny with a perfect white stripe around its middle lift its tail and pee right in the middle of Ralph and Sheila's white down comforter.

Sheila screams. Ralph lets out a string of curse words that I can't repeat. Nana and Papa exchange amused looks. Libby runs over and grabs the baby. And I just start laughing.

"You—" Sheila whirls around and points at Nana and Papa. "—you do not *ever* bring these—these criminals with you again. They are *not* invited!"

Nana sets her hands on her hips. Papa stands up tall.

"That's quite all right, Sheila," Papa says. "We won't be coming camping with you again. We'd much rather camp with the criminals."

🥕   🥕   🥕

We leave Ralph and Sheila stripping their sheets off their bed and head back to our campsite. I take the missing baby from Libby and she pushes the pet stroller with the other rabbits. Just as we come around the front of the RV, a small blue pickup truck pulls up beside us. The window rolls down and the lady from the farm leans over and says, "I got your note. I've been looking for you. I'd like my rabbits back."

Libby immediately bursts into tears. "Nana, Papa, please, don't make us give them back! *Ple-e-e-ase!* She's going to *ea-ea-eat* them!"

The lady sighs and shakes her head. "I am *not* going to eat them."

Libby wipes her nose. "You—you're not?"

"No. I'm not," the lady says with a weary, but kind, smile. "It's true, we did get Hasenpfeffer planning to breed her for meat. We've never had rabbits before, but all the hobby farm websites and magazines talk about how they're the ultimate sustainable meat source, so we thought we'd give it a try. But now that she's had her first litter, neither my husband nor I can bring ourselves to harvest them. They're just too darned cute."

"You're really not going to eat them then?" Libby says.

"No." The lady laughs. "I promise you, we aren't."

"Then what will you do with them?" I ask.

"Find them good homes, I hope. I've got a sign up by the highway. Didn't you see it? 'Baby bunnies for sale.'"

"Uh, no." I glance at Libby, who's now looking pretty embarrassed.

"I think I saw that sign," Papa says. "It's got a large red arrow pointing down Mackenzie Beach Road."

"That's the one." The lady nods.

"Well, Libby," Nana says. "I guess you went to all that bother of rescuing them for nothing."

Libby's cheeks are growing redder and redder. "I'm sorry," she says.

"Y'know," I say. "I think I know somebody who's looking for a baby bunny."

"Not you," Nana says, frowning.

I shake my head. "No, Sam! She was going to talk to her dad, remember?"

"Oh, yes!" Libby nods. "Sam wants the one Drew's holding. She wants to name him Oreo."

"Well, then send her my way," the lady says.

"What about Hasenpfeffer?" I ask. I think about poor Hasenpfeffer, all alone in that hutch after her babies are given new homes.

"She could live in your house," Libby suggests. "She would like that."

"I don't think so. My husband would never permit it. Animals live outside." The lady chuckles. "We'll find a home for her, too. No reason to keep her now."

"Come on," Papa says. "Let's get these bunnies back to their barn."

The lady has a metal cage in the back of her truck, the kind they use at the rabbit show at the Agri-Fair every summer. She gets out of the truck and holds the cage door open while we put the rabbits inside. Hasenpfeffer thumps when we put her in, then settles down and begins sniffing and licking her babies.

"Aw, it's like she's kissing them," Libby says. "Can't we keep just one? Please, please, please?"

Nana gives her a look that says she'd rather wade through hot lava first.

"Bye, bunnies. Good luck with your new homes," I

say as the lady shuts the cage, closes the back of the truck, and hops into the cab and drives away.

"Well," Papa says. "I hope the pair of you learned something today."

"I did," I say. "Don't go camping with Sheila!"

Nana stifles a laugh, then gives both me and Libby a stern look. "Not quite. How about not jumping to conclusions? Not taking things that don't belong to you? Staying off other people's property without their permission?" She ticks each item off on her fingers.

"Uh, yeah," I say. "Definitely learned that stuff, too."

"I'm really sorry, Nana." Libby stares at her feet. "We just wanted to save the bunnies."

I scowl at her. "*You* wanted to save the bunnies."

"Well, you both made some very foolish choices and I think you need to spend this morning thinking about them." Nana sets her hands on her hips.

"So I guess it's not a good time to ask to go to the beach?"

"Most definitely not a good time."

Figured.

23
Rabbits Don't Fall in Love

Libby and I spend the morning stuck at the campsite, even though the beach is right there beside us, just begging for us to come play. Papa gets a call from the hardware store that the toilet part is there. So he goes and gets it and sets to work fixing the toilet. Nana decides the trailer needs cleaning and pulls out a mop and bucket and a pair of rubber gloves. Ralph and Sheila seem to have decided to go home early. They're packing up all their gear into their RV. How they make it fit, I'll never know. But they manage to cram everything into it, then they hook up their car to the back, climb in, and roar off in a cloud of dust.

Tiny's cage needs cleaning, so Libby and I work on that. We put Tiny in his harness and tie his leash to the picnic table. He sniffs around a bit, then finds a shady spot and lies down. While Libby holds a garbage bag, I dump out the dirty shavings.

"Ew, shavings stink!" Libby says.

"You got that right." I hold my nose. No wonder people think rabbits stink. At home we use wood pellets in Tiny's litter box and it barely smells.

I'm washing the bottom of the cage out with the hose at the back of the trailer when Sam stops by. She's dressed in her bathing suit and has a boogie board under her arm.

"Drew, your girlfriend's here," Libby says.

"For the bazillionth time, she is *not* my girlfriend!" I say.

Sam rolls her eyes. "We're just friends, Libby."

"Friends who *kiss*!"

"Here, Libby, dry this." I hand her the cage bottom, slopping some water onto her shirt.

"Drew!"

"Whoops!"

Libby sticks her tongue out at me, but takes the dripping cage bottom and starts drying it with a beach towel.

"So you guys going to the beach?" Sam asks.

"We're kinda grounded."

"Grounded?"

"Yeah." I sigh and tell her the whole story. How Libby convinced me to rescue the rabbits, how we hid them in Ralph and Sheila's RV, and then how we got caught and had to give the bunnies back.

"Wow."

"Yeah."

"So no beach?"

"No beach." I sigh.

"Oh, hey! You'll never guess what?" Sam says. "Daddy says I can have a bunny!"

"That's great!" I grin at her. "I told the lady you might get one."

"So they're really for sale?"

"Yup."

"Maybe I'll hit the beach later," she says, with a laugh. "Gonna see if Daddy wants to go look at bunnies. I'll catch you later."

"Sure thing."

"Is she getting a bunny?" Libby asks after Sam leaves.

"I think so."

Libby squeals and claps her hands. "I'm so excited, Drew. I hope she remembers everything I told her."

"I'm sure she does," I say. "Sam's smart."

"Are you two going to get married?"

"Libby!"

"Just asking!"

"Are you finished drying that yet?" I sigh.

Libby hands me the plastic cage bottom and we fill it with shavings and attach the metal cage top. I fill the water bowl and pellet dish. Then Libby goes to untie the rabbit's leash. "Okay, Tiny. Time to go back into your cage."

But Tiny's not there.

Just like karaoke night, Tiny's leash has been chomped in half and Tiny is nowhere to be seen. Not again!

"Tiny!" Libby cries. "Oh, Tiny! What did you do?"

"We'll find him!" I say.

We search the campsite, under the truck and the trailer, in the bushes between our site and Ralph and Sheila's, up and down the road, we even run out onto the beach and check there. No Tiny.

"You don't think—?" Libby says.

"He wouldn't have—" I say. "He couldn't have—"

We race to the trailer door.

"Nana! Papa! We have to go to the lady's farm!"

"What?" Nana comes to the door, mop in hand. "Why? You know she's—"

I cut her off. "Tiny! He's gone again!"

"And you think he's gone there?"

"Where else would he go?"

"What's this about Tiny?" Papa calls from the bathroom.

"He's missing!" Libby says. "Again!"

"Hang on." Nana tosses her gloves aside and grabs the key to the truck. "Okay, let's go."

We hop in and head up the road to the farm. Penny greets us halfway down the drive with her loud woofing and leads the truck up to the house.

"I thought I might see you," the lady says, coming out onto the porch. She takes us out to the barn and sure enough, there's Tiny in the same hutch as before, lying side by side with Hasenpfeffer with only the wire mesh between them.

"He showed up about ten minutes ago."

"He sure seems to like your farm," I say.

"No," Libby says. "He wants to be with Hasenpfeffer. He loves her."

"Now, Libby," Nana says. I can tell she's getting impatient. "Rabbits don't fall in love."

"Yes, they do! It's called bonding. You can't separate them once they're bonded. They'll die of a broken heart!"

"Where on earth did you hear that?"

"It's true," I say. "That's what *The Ultimate House Rabbit Guide Book* says."

"But how can they be bonded? They've barely just met!"

"Maybe it's love at first sight," I say. "He was in the cage beside her all night."

"That's long enough," Libby nods.

"I don't know much about rabbit bonding," the lady says, "but he does seem to have taken a shine to Hasenpfeffer, and she to him."

Through the wire mesh, Hasenpfeffer is grooming the fur on one of Tiny's giant ears.

"We can't up and bring home another rabbit!" Nana says. "Not without your parents' permission. What would they say?"

"Then let's call them!" Libby says. "Where's your phone?"

Nana glances at her watch. "Oh, I don't know if that's a good idea. There's a three-hour difference. They're probably not even awake yet."

"Text them?" I say. "Send an email?"

Nana sighs and pulls out her phone. She taps a short text message into it and flips it closed. "It might be a while before they respond. Let's just get Tiny and take him back to the campsite. We'll see what they say when we hear from them."

The lady opens Tiny's hutch and I pull him out. He doesn't seem so eager to see me this time. Hasenpfeffer's nose is pressed to the wire mesh on the door of her hutch. She looks rather unhappy that Tiny is leaving.

"But, Nana—" Libby says.

Just then "It's a Small World" starts playing loudly in Nana's purse.

"It's them!" Libby cries, rushing to help Nana open her purse.

"Thank you, Libby. I can manage." Nana pulls the phone out. "Oh, hi, Todd. I didn't think you'd be up yet

... No, no emergency. We just ... Well, we have a bit of a problem ... with Tiny.... No, nothing like that. He's fine. He's just, well, he's decided he wants a friend. Libby calls it bonding? ... Well, I don't know how it happened. He got out ... It's rather a long story ... To make it short, he's found himself a friend and Libby assures me he'll die if we don't take the other bunny home with us.... What? Oh, hi, Jessica.... Yes, bonded. Libby assures me they are. They were cuddling in the hutch just now.... It's a bit of a story ... Yes, a female. You sure? Oh, well, then in that case ... Okay ... Okay, we'll see you tomorrow. Safe flight home. Bye." She clicks the phone closed.

Libby and I stare at her.

"Well, what did she say?" I prod.

Nana sighs and takes out her wallet. "How much did you want for her?" she asks the lady.

Libby cheers so loud it makes Hasenpfeffer thump.

🥕 🥕 🥕

Papa gapes like a fish out of water when he sees us come back with two rabbits. "Didn't we already return that one?" he says, pointing to Hasenpfeffer.

"Mom says we can keep her!" Libby says.

Nana sighs. "It would seem Tiny has fallen in love and will die without his new bride."

"It's called bonding," I say.

225

Papa just shakes his head.

Tiny's cage is still sitting on the ground by the picnic table. We put the rabbits inside. If the cage was too small for Tiny, it's definitely too small for both rabbits. They can barely turn around without bumping into each other. They don't seem to mind, though. They're too busy snuggling, cheek to cheek.

"They're going to need a bigger cage," I say.

"This will have to do," Nana says. "It's just for one night."

I help Papa carry the cage into the trailer. Libby gets some vegetables out of the fridge. She feeds some parsley to the rabbits. Tiny grabs one end of a stem, Hasenpfeffer the other end, and they munch towards each other.

Libby gasps. "Aw! Look! It's just like *Lady and the Tramp*!"

Sickening.

We watch the rabbits for a while. They really do look like they're in love. When they finish eating, Tiny licks Hasenpfeffer's forehead. She pushes her head under his chin, closes her eyes, and tooth-purrs.

"Hasenpfeffer seems really happy," I say.

Libby wrinkles her nose. "She needs a new name."

I have to agree. "Who names a rabbit after stew?"

"I know!" Libby says. "Sparkles!"

"No way! That is a dumb name!"

"No, you're dumb!"

"Now, now, kids. No squabbling," Nana says, opening her purse. "Flip a coin?"

"But she got to name Tiny!" I say.

"You said you didn't care what I called him!"

"This time I do!"

Nana hands me a quarter.

With a sigh, I take the coin from her and flip it into the air. "Call it."

"Heads!"

This time it's tails. All right!

"So what's it going to be?" Papa says.

To be honest, I have no idea what to call her. Just *not* Sparkles. "I'll have to think about it."

"She looks like a Smudge or a Speckles to me," Nana says. "Or maybe even a Freckles."

"No." I shake my head. Too much like Sparkles.

"What about Flopsy or Lopsy?" Libby says.

"No way." At least she hasn't suggested Precious. Ugh.

"Hasenpfeffer literally means 'hare pepper.' Maybe call her Pepper?" Papa suggests.

I tap my chin. "She doesn't really look like a Pepper."

"Daisy? Buttercup? Rosemary?" Nana says.

Hasenpfeffer nibbles another stem of parsley. It disappears into her mouth like it's being pulled in by a tractor beam.

227

"What about Parsley?" I say.

"Oh! I like Parsley," Libby says. "Tiny and Parsley! Parsley and Tiny! They go good together."

"What do you think?" I kneel down to scratch Hasenpfeffer on the nose. "Do you want to be Parsley?"

She nose bumps my hand.

"I think it suits her," Nana says.

"Work for me," Papa adds.

"Okay then." I give Parsley's nose a good rub. "Nice to meet you, Parsley Rabbit."

"Parsley *Sparkles* Rabbit," Libby says.

"Libby!"

"*Please?*"

I sigh. "Fine."

"Well," Nana says. "This has been quite the day and it's not even noon!"

"Quite the week, actually," Papa says.

Nana laughs and shakes her head. "Yes, quite the week. I really hope you two have learned something from all this."

"Oh, we have," I say. "At least *I* have."

"Me, too, Nana." Libby nods.

"Well, I'm glad to hear that."

"Does this mean we can go to the beach?" I say hopefully.

"Yes, I think that means you can go to the beach."

This time I cheer so loud it makes the rabbits thump.

24
Naughty Rabbit

While Nana makes us some lunch, Papa finishes fixing the toilet. I hear a flush and run to the bathroom to see. Papa is standing there, watching the last of the mucky brown water swirl down the drain.

"It works?" I say.

"It works!" He grins at me.

I could cheer again.

Just then there's a knock at the trailer door. Sam is there. And she's got a baby bunny in her arms. The one with the white stripe around his middle. The one who peed on Ralph and Sheila's bed. He's wearing a tiny red harness with a red leash attached.

"Meet Oreo!" she says.

"Yay!" Libby squeals. "You got a bunny!"

"Yup. Just got back from the pet shop with all his stuff. You guys should come check out his setup. I think you'd be proud. I got him an exercise pen and a pet tent with a tunnel that he just loves running up and down."

"Did you get him hay?" Libby asks.

"Yup. Got lots of hay."

"Speaking of hay," I say. "Tiny hasn't had any grass today. We should take the rabbits to the park later."

"Oh, that would be fun!" Sam says.

"We can bring Parsley!" Libby says.

"Parsley?" Sam says.

"Hasenpfeffer," I say.

"Oh!" Sam says. "The lady said someone bought Hasenpfeffer."

"Yup," I say. "We did."

"Parsley," Libby says. "Her name is Parsley now."

"I definitely like that better." Sam smiles, showing off her braces. "I'm sure we can bring them all. You've got the pet stroller, right?"

Together we map out a plan for later.

"Okay, kids," Nana says. "You better get something to eat."

"Day's a-wasting." Papa nods.

"We're going to the beach!" Libby says.

"You're not grounded?"

"Not anymore!"

"Great! I'll take Oreo back to the campsite and get

my boogie board." Sam waves and heads off.

Libby and I gobble up our lunch. Then we get changed into our bathing suits. Papa gets out a beach umbrella and a small cooler from one of the storage cubbies under the trailer. Nana packs the cooler with some cold drinks. Then we each grab a lawn chair and a beach towel and head out onto the sand. We find a spot above the high tide mark and set up our stuff.

"I'm going to build a sandcastle," Libby says. "Can you help, Papa?"

"Of course!" He grins at her. "You're looking at a regular sandcastle architect."

Nana pulls out a tattered paperback and makes herself comfortable in the shade of the umbrella.

I head straight for the water. The first wave that hits me feels cold, but the sun is hot so it's refreshing instead of shocking. I wade out until I'm about waist deep. The waves are almost over my head. I jump when they come rolling in so the water doesn't splash me in my face.

A few minutes later, Sam comes running down the beach. She's got two boogie boards.

"I borrowed Daddy's for you," she says.

"Thanks!" I grin at her. Could I have made a better friend?

The rest of the afternoon is awesome. We play in the waves for hours. We have a sandcastle building contest with Libby. Papa lets us bury him in the sand. I find a big piece of kelp and chase the girls with it. Then Sam finds an even bigger piece of kelp and they chase me. Nana has brought a bag of chips and some dip, so we take a break and have a snack. Then Sam and I go back to playing in the waves, going further and further out until Nana and Papa and Libby look like specks on the beach.

Eventually, the adults wave us back in.

"It's almost seven," Nana says. "You must be starving. Time to get some dinner."

"Can we come back to the beach after?" I ask. This afternoon went by way too fast.

"What about the bunnies?" Libby says. "I thought we were going to take them to the park?"

Oh, right. I almost forgot. "I guess Tiny's probably starving by now."

"And Parsley, too!"

"I'll meet you guys there?" Sam says, taking the boogie boards.

I nod and she trots off down the beach.

We pack up our stuff and head back to the campsite.

Papa holds the trailer door open for us and we troop inside.

I stop short. There is rabbit poop all over the floor and two orange puddles of pee. The cage is wide open. Tiny and Parsley are cuddled up on the couch, nose to nose.

Uh oh.

"My floors! I just washed them!" Nana squeaks.

"Get those rabbits back in their cage!" Papa growls.

I catch Parsley easily enough. She doesn't even try to run. But Tiny, of course, doesn't want to go back in his cage. He runs under my bunk and won't come out.

"Come on, Tiny," I say. "It's just for a little while longer. We're going home tomorrow."

"Let me try, Drew," Libby says. She's got a piece of carrot. Tiny takes one look at it and comes hopping out. I scoop him up and pop him into the cage with Parsley. Libby gives him the carrot. She's gives a piece to Parsley, too. "We'll go eat some grass at the park soon!" Libby says, scratching both rabbits behind the ears.

233

"But not before you give these floors a proper cleaning." Nana hands me the mop and broom and Libby the dustpan and a bucket.

Ugh.

We sweep up the poops and throw them in the garbage, then I mop up the pee off the floor.

"Do a good job," Nana says.

"Yes, Nana."

RATTLE! RATTLE! Tiny has finished his piece of carrot and has decided he wants back out. He grabs the latch on the door and gives it a good shake. *RATTLE! RATTLE! CLANG!* The latch gives and the door swings open. Tiny hops out, followed by Parsley.

"Oh!" Nana cries.

"Well, I'll be." Papa raises his eyebrows.

"That explains a lot," I say.

"See, Drew! I *told* you I didn't let him out!" Libby says.

🥕 🥕 🥕

After dinner, Sam is waiting for us at the park with Oreo on his leash. He's hopping around, sniffing everything and doing little happy binky hops much the same way Tiny did when he was that age. Several kids have gathered around Sam and are oohing and aahing over the bunny.

"Where did you get him?"

"How old is he?"

"What's his name?"

"I want a bunny, too!"

Then they spot us and run over. "Hey, Tiny's here!"

"Tiny! Yay!"

Our rabbit has reached celebrity status.

"Oh, wow! You've got another bunny!"

"It looks just like Sam's bunny!"

"Where did you get him?"

"This is Oreo's mom," Libby says.

"Are there more babies?"

"Can I pet her?"

"I want a bunny, too!"

"The lady at the farm up the road has the other babies," Libby says. "We got Parsley from her."

"I'm going to ask if I can have a bunny!"

"Me too!"

Several kids run off to their campsites.

Oh boy. We've opened a real can of worms.

"Libby, is it smart to tell all these kids about the baby bunnies? You don't know if they'll give them good homes."

Libby frowns. "The lady said she'd find them good homes."

"She will," Sam says. "You should've heard the list of questions she asked me and Daddy before she let us take Oreo."

"See, Drew!" Libby crosses her arms.

"Okay, okay."

We let Tiny out of the stroller. His leash is pretty short now, it's got so many knots in it to hold it together, but he doesn't seem to mind. He nose-bumps Oreo, then starts gobbling grass like crazy. Parsley doesn't have a harness or leash, so she stays in the stroller. She doesn't seem to mind, though. I think after living in that hutch for so long, the big wide world scares her. Libby picks some grass and feeds it to her through the zippered opening. She gobbles the grass up as fast as Tiny. We're going to need a bigger lawn at home.

We plop down on the grass and let the rabbits eat. I kick off my flip-flops and lie back. Above me, puffy white clouds are slowly moving overhead, leaving the ocean behind and heading for the mainland. High above some sea gulls are catching the wind currents. I pull my hat over my eyes and just enjoy the warm sun rays.

More kids swarm around to see the bunnies. Libby and Sam answer tons of questions. Finally, the kids run out of things to ask and wander off to play.

"Come on, Drew," Sam says. "Let's go play some Frisbee." She hands Oreo's leash to Libby and grabs her Frisbee.

"Sure thing." I stuff my feet into my flip-flops, stand up, and run after Sam. At least that's what I try to do.

Instead I trip over my own feet and land face first in the grass. *THUD!* Ouch.

Sam giggles. "You okay, Drew?"

"Yeah." I clamber to my feet, try to take a step, and nearly fall on my face again. What the—? I glance down at my feet. The plastic thong between my toes on my right foot has been chomped in half.

I groan. The rabbit ate my flip-flops.

25

The Whole Story

The next morning after breakfast, we pack up the trailer, say our goodbyes to Gord and Brenda, pile into the truck, and head back home. I've got Sam's Skype ID written on a piece of paper in my pocket. She's promised she'll message me as soon as she gets home. I've promised to do the same. She says she'll send me Oreo updates and wants me to send her news about Tiny and Parsley. It's going to be weird not seeing her every day. Thank goodness for modern technology.

As soon as we pull out on the highway, Nana says, "Who wants some music?"

"Me!" Libby cries.

"Please, no!" I groan.

Too late. Nana slides the CD into the player and music fills the cab. Then it starts skipping like crazy.

"Oh my!" Nana says and ejects the CD. "Oh dear. It looks like it got too much sun." She holds up the CD, showing us the weird distorted rainbow on the bottom side.

"Too bad," I say.

"We could sing!" Libby says. "Like karaoke!" She starts belting out the song she sang on karaoke night. Made-up words and all.

Ugh.

When we get to Cathedral Grove, Papa stops the truck and we climb out. For the next hour we wander the paths, gazing up at the huge trees, just as in awe as when we did the rainforest hike. Only today it's not freezing cold and raining. Nana takes our picture in front of a huge tree. And this time I don't hide.

We drive to Port Alberni. "I'm sure glad there wasn't a tsunami," Libby says.

Me too. We had enough trouble this trip without a natural disaster, too.

As promised, we stop for lunch in Coombs.

"Oh, look at the goats! They're so cute!" Libby says. "Just think if they had rabbits on the roof!"

"When you grow up," Papa says. "You can start your own market and put rabbits on the roof."

Probably not a good idea to encourage her. I can tell by the dreamy look on her face, she's already making plans.

We check on Tiny and Parsley. They're still in their cage. Tiny doesn't look impressed. Papa found a metal clip in his toolbox and attached it to the door latch. Try as he might, Tiny can't open it. I give him a scratch on the nose. "We'll be home soon, Tiny. Then no more cages for you."

In a few hours, we pull up in front of our house and climb out. It feels like forever since we've been gone.

Mom and Dad come out the front door to greet us. Their flight home was last night.

Libby runs up the walk and throws herself into Mom's arms. "I missed you, Mommy!"

"Me, too," Mom says, hugging Libby like she'll never let her go again.

Dad ruffles my hair. "Glad to be home?" he asks me.

Am I ever!

"So?" Nana says. "How was Hawaii?"

"Terrible." Mom shakes her head. "First our flight was delayed by several hours because someone got sick on the plane while we were still on the runway. Then our luggage didn't show up for two days. The air conditioner in our hotel room didn't get cold. The pool was closed. And Todd got stung by a jellyfish." She sighs.

"Oh dear," Nana says. "Well, I hope you were still able to enjoy yourself a little bit."

Mom considers. "Well, the food was good and the conference was fantastic. So it wasn't all bad."

"It could've been a lot worse," Dad agrees.

"I'm just glad to be home." Mom shakes her head.

"How about you guys?" Dad asks. "How was your camping trip?"

Nana and Papa exchange looks. "Well ..."

"It was great!" I say. "We went to the beach, we made s'mores, we saw some of the hugest trees, I rode my bike, and I made a new friend."

"*And* we got a new bunny!" Libby says.

"Oh, yes," Mom says. "Let's meet her."

"You will love her," Libby says. "She's such a nice bunny."

Papa opens the trailer and Libby and I introduce Mom and Dad to Parsley. We tell them the whole story of how we found her and how we ended up keeping her. I try to leave a few parts out, but Papa raises his eyebrows at me, so I have to include them.

"So you *stole* rabbits—" Dad says, a scowl forming on his face.

"Rescued, Daddy," Libby corrects him. "We rescued them."

"Rabbits that didn't even *need* rescuing," Dad says, his face is starting to turn that shade of red it always does when he gets mad.

"We didn't know that," I mumble.

"We thought she was going to eat them!" Libby says.

"Whatever your intentions were, Libby, when you

take something that's not yours, it's stealing." Mom crosses her arms. "You're lucky she didn't call the police."

Dad shakes his head. "You weren't even supposed to take one rabbit camping, let alone come home with two."

Libby stares at the ground. "I just wanted to save them."

"You've got a good heart, honey," Mom says. "But you need to use your head, too."

"What I don't get," Dad says. "Is why you would help her, Drew?"

"I, uh," I stammer.

"I made him do it," Libby says. "He didn't want to. He tried to stop me. But I didn't listen."

Mom sighs.

Dad sighs.

"You won't make us take her back, will you?" Libby's lower lip is starting to wobble. "Tiny will die. Parsley will die, too. They're bonded."

"No, Libby. We won't take her back." Mom says. "We're just very disappointed with you two."

"I'm really sorry they were so much trouble," Dad says to Nana and Papa.

"Don't be too hard on them, Todd," Papa says. "I think they've both learned some valuable lessons."

"Do you even remember some of the mischief you

and your brother used to get up to when we went camping?" Nana says. "Like the year you nearly started a forest fire? It's a good thing the local fire department was having their annual picnic that day. You could've burned down the whole campground."

"It was an accident," Dad says.

Papa chuckles. "Or when you two went around stealing marshmallows from all the neighbouring campsites?"

"We were trying to create the ultimate s'more."

"Or what about the time we caught you setting off bottle rockets in the outhouse toilets?" Nana shakes her head. "Pe-ew!"

"That was Shawn's idea!" Dad is turning red again, but this time it's not the angry red.

"I was sure the two of you were going to send me to an early grave." Nana shakes her head.

"Wow!" I say. "I had no idea you got into so much trouble as a kid."

"What did Ralph and Sheila do?" Libby asks.

"Oh, this was long before we met Ralph and Sheila," Papa says. "They didn't join in on our annual camping trip until your dad was in college."

"Ralph and Sheila? Aren't they the ones who organize all your trips?" Dad asks.

"Not anymore." Nana shakes her head. "From now on, we'll be taking care of that on our own."

"Oh?"

"Let's just say, they don't know how to camp with kids." Nana chuckles.

"Well," Papa says. "I guess we better get going if we plan to get this rig home before dark."

We unload our bags from the truck, take my bike down from the back of the trailer, and lift out the rabbit cage. Tiny rattles the bars.

"I know, Tiny," I say. "You want out."

Libby and I hug Nana and Papa goodbye.

"Thanks so much for taking us camping," I say. "We had a good time."

"Me too," Libby says.

"Did you really?" Papa says.

I nod. "Yes! I mean, except for the getting in trouble part."

Papa laughs his booming laugh. "Yes, I can see that part not being a lot of fun."

"So would you like to come camping with us again next summer?" Nana asks.

"You bet!" I say.

"Can we bring Tiny and Parsley?" Libby asks. "Tiny *loves* camping."

"Well ..." Nana says, glancing at Papa. "We'll have to talk about that."

While Libby and Dad and Mom get Parsley settled in, I drag my suitcase upstairs, dump the contents on my bed, dig out my iPod and plug it in. Then I boot up my computer and sign in to Skype. I add Sam to my contacts. Then check to see if Quentin is online. He is.

Me: DUDE!

Qchow99: Sup?

Me: I'm back!

Qchow99: Oh hey! Did u have fun camping?

Me: Not at first. But I did at the end.

Qchow99: Cool

Me: So is Galaxy Guilds totally awesome?

Qchow99: Don't know

Me: What? Why?

Qchow99: Not out yet

Me: What?

Qchow99: Its delayed

Me: What?

Qchow99: DELAYED

Me: I got that. Why?

Qchow99: Don't know

Me: When does it launch?

Qchow99: Tomorrow

Me: No way.

Qchow99: Yes way

Me: So I totally didn't miss anything?
Qchow99: Nope

I sit back in my computer chair. I can hardly believe it. I'd been so bummed out thinking I was going to miss out on a week of Galaxy Guilds and it hasn't even launched yet.

Unbelievable.

Me: I gotta unpack.
Qchow99: K
Me: Galaxy Guilds tomorrow?
Qchow99: TOTALLY!
Me: :)
Qchow99: Cya

I close Skype and practically dance around my room.

"Drew! Drew!" Libby calls from downstairs. "Come see Tiny and Parsley! Aw! They're so cute!"

"Yeah, coming!" I yell back.

It's kinda crazy we now have two rabbits. I think back over the past week and everything that's happened. One thing's for sure. We don't need to worry about Tiny being lonely ever again.

"Oh, and, um, Drew?" Libby calls again. "Parsley peed on your shoes!"

I sigh. Then I groan. Then I laugh.

Acknowledgements

Thanks to my friends and family, whose support means so much to me. Thanks to those who've helped contribute to making this book a reality, especially Linda Au Parker and Deanna Dionne. Also thanks to groups like Rabbitats Rabbit Rescue for their tireless work in education, advocacy, and rescue of unwanted and neglected rabbits. And lastly, thanks goes to the many writers groups I've been a part of over the years—everyone at Backspace, the SCWBI Blueboards, the KBoards, CritClub, the In the Middle Critters, MG Buddies, and various other private groups—for your guidance, comradery, and kicks in the butt.

About the Author

Rachel Elizabeth Cole writes a mix of genres, from heartfelt to humorous, but her favourite will always be middle grade fiction. When she's not writing, Rachel works as a graphic designer specializing in book covers. Her favourite season is autumn, she prefers tea to coffee, and wishes every morning began at ten a.m. Even though she hates the rain, Rachel lives just outside Vancouver, British Columbia, with her husband, their two sons, and two very spoiled house rabbits.

Find out more at *www.rachelelizabethcole.com*

Made in the USA
Monee, IL
01 December 2024

71485896R00152